At Bonus Time,

No-one Can Hear You Scream

AT BONUS TIME, NO-ONE CAN HEAR YOU SCREAM

◆ ◆

David Charters

◆

Photographs by
Alice Rosenbaum

Elliott & Thompson
London

Author's Note and Acknowledgements

'Bonus Time' started life as a short story, but never knew when to stop growing. My publishers encouraged me to give it full rein and you have before you the result. It is not so much a chronicle of a particular time in the City of London, as the exploration of a type of character and the way that character responds to the extraordinary pressures placed upon people in the extreme situations that the City produces. Among my former colleagues, even the most ruthlessly aggressive fall short of Dave Hart and his fellows. Bartons, their bank, is not modelled on any single British merchant bank, but rather draws together the worst features of the scramble to emulate the Americans, borrowing the ugliest aspects of the soulless finance factories of Wall Street, while missing the lessons that the best US investment banks could have offered to help ensure an independent future for more British firms.

Alice Rosenbaum brings a whole new perspective on the City, capturing the familiar and the human alongside the giant and impersonal, whether in the architecture of the Square Mile or the lifestyles of its workforce. She is a subtle and astute observer of the world around us.

I am grateful as ever to a number of people for their help and input: Lorne Forsyth, John McLaren and Nick Webb deserve special mention, as well as Gavin Henderson of Laidlaw Capital. My oldest son, Mark, gave comments and insight, and most of all my wife Luisa kept the whole show on the road, as always.

Last night I killed my boss. It was the second time this week, only this time it was much worse. He was sitting at his desk in his big, glass-sided, corner office, looking out at the trading floor with its hundreds of identical workstations, the computer screens, the phones, and us, the worker bees who feed the machine. Looking at us, as we stayed late in the run-up to the annual bonus round, putting in face time to look good, keeping busy, trying to persuade him how essential we all were. Well, I'd had enough. I wasn't essential anymore – at least I didn't feel as if I was – and I was going to act before someone took the decision for me.

I cough nervously, glance around at my colleagues who all have their eyes glued to the screens in front of them, and pick up my briefcase from under my desk, leaving my jacket over the back of my chair. Now, this may sound straightforward, but you don't normally carry your briefcase around the trading floor unless you're going home, and when you go home, you put your jacket on. But if I put my jacket on first – at this time of year – the rest of the team will look at me and I don't want to attract attention, not at this stage.

So I leave my jacket but pick up my briefcase and walk in a lopsided way, half hiding it in front of me as I make my way to his office with my back to the team.

I step inside the open door and close it behind me. I reach across and pull the blinds, so we can't be seen from the floor. He looks up, puzzled.

'What are you doing?'

I smile, reassuring, ingratiating.

'Rory, there's… something I wanted to discuss with you.'

He sighs and looks at his watch. 'Okay, I'll give you five minutes, but do me a favour – no more special pleading about the bonus, okay?'

'No, no more special pleading, Rory.' I smile again, a little nervously – still in character – and open my briefcase on his desk, but with the lid facing him so he can't see what I'm taking out. 'In fact no pleading at all.'

I close the lid with a firm click and swing a sixteen-inch machete up in the air.

Now, before you say anything, a sixteen-inch machete may not seem much, but it had to fit into my briefcase, which is not large. Even in London you can't just go and buy a full-sized machete without attracting some degree of attention. As I like to think I'm a little smarter than some mere criminal on the street, I'd bought the machete at auction, at Christie's, along with a collection of other memorabilia of famous nineteenth century explorers in Africa. So when I swing it through a broad arc and bring it down with a thunk into the middle of Rory's perfectly coiffed, fair-haired, blue-eyed skull, I'm actually using a piece of history.

The problem is, it gets stuck. The weapon goes *thunk,* right into his head, splintering the bone. My arm is driven by the strength that can only come from years of resentment, humiliation, nervous anxiety, pitiful gratitude and festering anger. He keels over, gently and silently, his eyes roll upwards and he bumps his head on his desk with a sigh. Seeing him lying there, helpless, I put one hand on his head and struggle to wrench the machete free for a second go (and to be honest, for a third and a fourth – I'd worked for Rory a long time).

And then he gets up! No kidding, he actually shakes his head, causing me to leap backwards, my eyes wide with fear and disbelief. He pulls himself together, lifts himself up from the desk, blood streaming down his face, eyes wide open, with the machete still sticking out of his skull. He comes round the desk towards me.

'You always were a loser.' His words have an icy venom to them – which I suppose is understandable. 'A loser, a no hoper, a truly second rate, sub-standard investment banker. The clients don't even like you, let alone respect you, half of them only deal with you out of sympathy, and you have no future here or at any other firm.' He jabs his finger in my chest to emphasise the points, and as he finishes, he reaches up, taking hold of the machete, grasping the handle, and pulls it out of his head, allowing a stream of blood to come gushing out of the crack in his skull splashing down over his face onto the carpet. 'You can't do a damned thing right.' There's blood all over the machete as he hands it back to me, and more blood runs down his forehead and face, but it doesn't seem to bother him. 'Now get out of my office. I have work to do – including some key bonus re-calculations.' As he says this, he gives me a long, meaning-ful stare – one of the ones I always hate, because when someone looks at you like that, you just know they've found you out – and then he flicks a drop of blood off the end of his nose and goes back to his desk.

When I get back to my workstation, my shirt is sticking to my sides with sweat. I pull my handkerchief out and mop my brow. As I glance around, I catch the eye of some of the other team members.

'Brown-nosing again?'

'Looks like it didn't pay off.'

'Rory's got the measure of you.'

And I start screaming. I scream so loud that I wake my wife.

'Darling – darling, are you all right?'

I shake my head to clear it, and reach for a glass of water from the bedside table. Wendy turns the light on.

'It was one of those awful dreams again, wasn't it?'

I nod, too shaken to speak.

'Oh, my darling,' she smiles, trying to be reassuring, and hugs me, though she clearly doesn't appreciate the sweat covering me from head to toe. 'Come on, darling – look on the bright side. It's not long now, is it? Then all this uncertainty will be over. It's… how many days?'

I glance at the clock on the bedside cabinet. Twelve thirty – half-an-hour after midnight, another day has started. 'Fifty-two days,' I gasp. 'Fifty-two days until we know.'

It was 6:30 in the morning. I was sitting on the tube, on the Circle Line to Monument, staring into space, working out what I'd do with a million pounds. Now, before you say anything, let me explain – even senior investment bankers take the tube sometimes. I know that Rory with his chauffeur-driven car would never be seen dead on the People's Underground, and why should he? He's the boss, after all. But for the rest of us, at least those who live in Chelsea, the journey into the City is quickest by Underground, especially first thing in the morning, even if it is a little democratic when it comes to things like getting a seat and who you rub shoulders with. And I know, I know – you don't need to say it. It's true that the man sitting next to me doesn't smell of Armani Mania. He smells of… well, let's just say he smells. And a lot of these people haven't even made their first million, and many of them never will. That's capitalism. It's enough for me that I know. I don't need to say anything.

But back to that million. We all know a million isn't what it used to be. To begin with, the Chancellor takes forty per cent. So a million is already six hundred thousand. Then the bank won't pay it all in cash. Probably half the balance will be in some form of share-based incentive – options, deferred shares, some weird derivative, or whatever. But it won't be cash and you can't spend it now – it only turns into folding money slowly, over a period of years, perhaps three or even five years, providing you stay at the bank and don't move to a competitor. If you do that, you lose it all. That's why they call these things golden handcuffs. So your actual cash in hand is perhaps three hundred thousand, and these days three hundred really doesn't go far.

Take an example. Have you any idea how much a Porsche costs? I thought not. Well the basic Boxster comes in at a mere £30k, but no-one, I mean no-one, serious can drive one of those in the Square Mile. The minimum is the 911 Turbo Cabriolet and for that you're talking the thick end of £100k. So already a big chunk of my bonus is gone.

I know what you're thinking – why buy a 911 at all? We already have a Range Rover – Vogue of course, with the usual extras – so why buy a second car? Well the thing is, we have to have the Range Rover. Wendy needs it to do the school run from our flat in Sloane Square to Cameron House, the private nursery school which Samantha attends, at the other end of the King's Road. It's almost half a mile, and kids these days need protection, and so does Wendy – not the world's greatest driver – so a big 4 X 4 is essential driving in Chelsea. It's also good for giving the impression that we have a place in the country, which we definitely don't yet, but would do if Rory ever got off his arse and gave me a decent bonus. And of course whenever Wendy ventures outside Chelsea, she needs protection even more – like when she takes Samantha to her Little Sweethearts ballet class in Fulham, or to her Young Prodigies violin lesson in Pimlico, her Gymnastics for Toddlers sessions in Battersea, or her Little Tadpoles swimming class in Putney. Don't laugh – if you don't do this stuff for your kids, they might not become a rock star, or Prime Minister, or win the Nobel Prize. Even White Van Man pulls over when he sees Wendy weaving down the middle of the road, talking on her mobile, staring into shop windows, at the wheel of a Range Rover.

But back to my car. We ought to be a two car family, because if I ever need to drive to the office, for example on a Sunday, I can't arrive in a Range Rover – at least not a clean one, the way they tend to be in Chelsea. At weekends Rory drives a DB7, but then he would, wouldn't he?

So once I've finally got myself a decent car of my own – a 911 Turbo Cabriolet – what else do I need? We still owe a hundred thousand on the mortgage on the flat, which we've paid down steadily over the past few years, and it would be satisfying to own it outright, but we already tell people we own it

ourselves, so there ought to be something more… demonstrable that flows from this year's bonus. We could think about a place in the country, but then people would expect to come and stay, and we simply don't have the kind of money you need to buy a place like Rory's: two hundred and fifty acres in Sussex, his own shoot, nine bedrooms, two guest cottages, five staff – you know the sort of thing. Or maybe you don't. Anyway, a cottage is definitely out of the question, even though in terms of strict space requirements, Wendy and I, and Samantha (who's three) could technically survive in a cottage – after all, we only have three bedrooms in Sloane Square. But it doesn't matter, because a million doesn't do it, so there's no point discussing it further.

Watches – and jewellery – always used to be a sure-fire sign of a successful bonus round, though these days people are getting more cynical. If Wendy and I treat ourselves to a new Rolex each, or better yet the latest Patek Philippe, people might think I really haven't done well and it's all a bluff.

We could re-decorate the flat. I haven't costed that, but one of those chi-chi interior designers could transform the place for us. The problem is, I sort of like it the way it is, and I'd hate the disruption of having to move out while a bunch of Polish builders and Croatian decorators moved in. And it always costs more and takes longer than they say – we pay Chelsea prices and get Warsaw delivery times.

If I only get a million, a few key purchases around the home are probably the best compromise – an antique dining table with chairs (less than £30k?), a new centrepiece picture for the drawing room (£20 – 25k?), a new set of crockery (£3 – 4K?) and perhaps new curtains (£10k?). We'd still have change for Barbados at Christmas, not forgetting the Porsche, and the balance I'd use to pay off the overdraft.

Overdraft? I can see the question in the thought bubble over your head. Well, yes, I do have an overdraft. I know what you're thinking. Why does a successful investment banker have an overdraft? Well, actually we all do.

No-one lives on their salary any more. Besides, Rory only pays me £100k a year, and Wendy couldn't begin to live on that. So what do you expect?

At 11:30 I had a meeting with the Finance Director of Pattison Construction. PC – as we call them on the team – is one of the biggest and fastest growing construction companies in the UK, having come from nowhere over the past five years. We took them public on the stockmarket two years ago, and now they've come to us for advice on what to do next. Yes, really – they've come to us for advice. It amazes me, but people still do that. Naturally, my advice is that they should do whatever will pay the bank the largest fees. In this case, I recommend we list their shares on the New York Stock Exchange, so that they can access US investors, increase liquidity in their shares and send their stock price higher. None of this is true, of course. The most serious US investors already can buy their shares, without the expense and trouble of a US listing. Creating a separate pool of shares in the US reduces liquidity, and in times of uncertainty, US investors would dump their shares pretty quickly and send the stock lower. But that's all detail. I like to think I'm a big picture man. The big picture I'm thinking of today is my bonus, because as you know, it's that time of year.

On reflection, any time of year is that time of year, but the last few weeks running up to bonus particularly so.

Anyway, PC nods, makes all the right noises and I orchestrate the presentation like a circus ringmaster. We explain why US investors have a different valuation approach to the construction sector and will push his stock higher, a representative of our US operation explains why our tiny New York office is best equipped to do the job (after all, why would anyone want to hire a US firm to do a job in the US?), and finally I wind up with my assurance of the firm's total commitment, how much we want the business, how great it will be for them, the strategic vision, the next step forward – sometimes I think I could do this stuff in my sleep. It's not that investment banking is undemanding work, it's just that at times it's repetitive. Like repeating the same script a hundred times. Or a thousand. I've been doing this a while now. In theory you get slicker, more persuasive, more reassuring, but it can come to sound... jaded. Not that I'd ever get bored with my job, of course. I'm committed, not quite in the way that lunatics get committed to an asylum, but committed nonetheless.

Afterwards, he tells me how impressed he is with our presentation, how highly he values our input, and how useful it is to be able to get genuinely sincere, impartial advice. For a moment I look at him and wonder if he's taking the piss, but then I realise he means it.

Christ, I'm good.

Wendy and I went to a dinner party at the Finkelsteins'. He runs the swaps desk at Hardman Stoney, one of the most successful US investment banks. He never has anything to say, always arrives at least half-an-hour late to his own dinner parties, and always looks distracted – almost vacant, though obviously that can't be right, because he runs the swaps desk at Hardman Stoney.

The Finkelsteins have an amazing apartment in Holland Park – the sort that Wendy dreams of. You come in through a grand reception area with marble floors and twenty-four hour porterage, step into a big mirror and marble elevator, and get out onto a large landing that serves just two apartments. You buzz at double doors, both of which open when your host's butler (hired for the night – don't worry, this isn't Rory's place) receives you and takes your coats.

The drawing room is huge, with a great view and interesting art: a contemporary bronze here, a classical marble bust there – you know the sort of thing. Or maybe not. Anyway, there are a few coffee tables and some couches, but mostly the impression is space and order. And a 'to die for' black babe dressed as a waitress offers you a drink with a 'come to bed and fuck me' smile on her face and a knowing look in her eyes. Where do they find these girls? Why can

Wendy only find short, fat Filipinas and Essex girls who claim to know what they're doing, but only spill things on guests, or worse yet, on the furniture?

Gloria Finkelstein is dressed from head to toe in Chanel – and it's wasted. Twenty thousand dollars, and you still can't defeat nature. That's without the hair stylist, the manicure, the pedicure, the botox, the lyposuction, the personal trainer, the masseur and the expensive suntan. I guess she must do something for Matt Finkelstein (or at least she did once upon a time). A few good memories and a killer of a pre-nuptial can do a hell of a lot for these American investment bankers' marriages.

Wendy on the other hand is wearing Donna Karan – a simple pale blue number to match her eyes that cost us a mere three thousand dollars on our last trip to New York. In Wendy's case it's the jewellery that does it – twenty thousand pounds' worth of 'heirlooms' for Samantha around her neck and wrists (that was how she justified them), mostly from Theo Fennel, with earrings from Elizabeth Gage: stunning, so much so that Gloria Finkelstein pays her the ultimate tribute of ignoring them, and compliments her instead on her new handbag (a mere three hundred pounds from Coach).

I take a glass of champagne from the black sex machine, ignoring Wendy's 'evil eye' and wonder what she would say if I offered her a thousand pounds to go to bed with me. I take a sip and discover – to my utter horror – that it's Krug. Not only that, but just in case I didn't notice, the bottle is sitting in an ice bucket on the sideboard, propped up so the label is on show. If that isn't typically crude one up-manship, I don't know what is. I make a mental note – next time Matt Finkelstein drops by, I must open a bottle of vintage Cristal. (Second mental note: order some).

We exchange the usual pleasantries: air kisses, compliments, how wonderful, it's been so long, you look amazing, how are the children, before we get

down to the real business of the evening (and this even before Matt Finkelstein has appeared!) – how are you doing? Sounds like a simple question, doesn't it? Except it doesn't really mean what it says. What it really means is (and at this point Wendy looks nervously in my direction, relenting on her previous irritation at my preoccupation with the black sex bomb): are you going to be paid more than my husband this year, and if so, what does it do to our relative positioning in the social pecking order?

Great, isn't it? As if it wasn't enough that the husbands compete, the wives have to do it too. My husband earns more than yours, he can buy me a bigger house/car/boat/holiday home and afford a better personal trainer/masseur/beautician/guru/tennis coach and we can spend even more money than you on exotic holidays/dinners at fancy restaurants/tickets to the boring fucking opera/weekend breaks in stately fucking homes and WE MUST BE FUCKING HAPPIER THAN YOU FUCKING LOSERS. Or something like that. And anyway, since we all do this stuff, it must be right.

Wendy does her best 'confident corporate wife', glancing at me, looking quietly confident, silently gratified at some hidden knowledge that she and I alone can share – I've been told something. Rory must have given me a hint. Obviously I can't say anything: everyone understands that. Especially Gloria. Wendy puts on such a good performance that we don't actually need to say anything. Gloria looks taken aback, perturbed, ever so slightly unsettled in a quite delicious way, and leaves us with unseemly haste when the bell rings to announce the next guests.

To my relief, it's the light entertainment. Gloria Finkelstein, ever the thoughtful hostess, has organised a Real Loser. He's here so we can all unite against him and reinforce our sense of security and permanence.

Joe Smith ran forward Foreign Exchange trading at SFP – Société Financière de Paris – until June last year. Then they closed down and pulled out of the London market. Not his fault, of course, his team was profitable, but that makes no difference: when he looks at me, and I look at him, we both know. Not that I'd ever say anything, of course. That's part of the fun.

Our wives know too. His wife, strangely known as Charly, is Hong Kong Chinese, and I've always had a soft spot for her – I bet she's a real goer. She's wearing a brightly coloured, vaguely oriental style, silk mini dress of indeterminate origin – oh dear, my dear, no label – with pearls – okay, I guess – and intricately patterned gold earrings that probably come from the Middle East – I bet they don't have hallmarks. She's in great shape, but that really isn't the point. I wonder what she would say if I offered her, oh, let's say ten grand – or maybe fifty, he's been unemployed for nearly a year now…

'Joe, how are you? And Charly, how wonderful to see you!'

Wendy and Gloria rush to embrace the arriving guests, revelling in their superiority. Sweetness and success: moments like this are what it's all about. But it's all relative – imagine what it feels like for a woman to be married to Rory.

Joe is embarrassed, trying not to be defensive, he has lots of possibilities, he's still exploring his options, obviously the market doesn't help – and yes, we all nod and no-one engages with him: because we don't have to, do we? He's a loser.

Before you say anything, I know it's not his fault – he ran a profitable, successful team, he made a lot of money for his firm, had a fearsome reputation in the market, and paid his people well, at least as long as they performed. It's not that he was kind, you understand. After all, kind is for girls. He was ambitious, aggressive, and like most of us, he knew how to smile upwards on the greasy career ladder and shit downwards. But he didn't have friends. Not that any of us do, really. But he made it particularly clear that he didn't care what his peers at other firms thought, and that was a mistake.

Most of us at least go through the motions, staying part of the 'club', because you never know when you might need a helping hand. Of course, for all I know, Joe's a loving, loyal husband and a wonderful father to his kids and helps small, furry woodland creatures in his spare time. But he's still a loser, and we know it and he knows it and Charly knows it too. He committed the Cardinal Sin: when he found himself in the wrong place at the wrong time, he had no friends and no Plan B. He was naked and alone with no-one to cry to, and when that happens, the City is a barren place – the sort of place that makes people become unravelled.

Just as the conversation is stretching out deliciously, reinforcing my sense of confidence and good fortune, Matt Finkelstein arrives and pops the bubble.

'Hi, I'm sorry, so sorry – we've just priced the biggest reverse forward equity swap with collars, caps and inverse reference prices that's ever been undertaken outside of the US.'

We all stare at him. Matt Finkelstein has zits. I know I shouldn't raise this now, just ahead of dinner, but if you were here you'd see them anyway. He's tall, skinny and is losing his hair. He would say he's lean, and it's true he does work out, in the special gym set aside for the use of Managing Directors only at Hardman Stoney. He would probably also say he's clever, and in a manner of speaking, that's true – though only in a narrow, specific way that wouldn't really help him; for instance if civilisation came to an end as the result of a nuclear holocaust and he had to fend for himself in the wild. Sure, he goes to the opera, but if you were to ask him who wrote *Tosca*, he'd gaze vacantly at you, say 'Huh?' and look around for some Eurotrash they'd hired on their graduate trainee programme to answer the question.

'Wow, Matt – fantastic! Congratulations. You must be over the moon.' I don't ask how profitable the trade was, because they don't necessarily know – these swaps guys are so smart, they bullshit their bosses every time they do a deal, book some huge notional profit for bonus purposes, and let their successors unwind the mess in a few years' time when it matures.

But the really clever thing about Matt's trade is that he's done it now. A dollar earned in the run-up to bonus is worth ten dollars earned at the beginning of the year. My last major success was back in March, which gives me a slightly sick feeling. I take a sip of Krug, but that only makes me feel worse.

'Why don't we go straight through and sit down?' Matt steers us through to the dining room, and can't help grinning as he sees the looks on our faces.

Their dining room has been transformed. They have a new centrepiece picture hanging over the fireplace – some contemporary splurge of colour that I'm sure we're all meant to recognise and must have cost a fortune, as well as a new dining suite, at least new to them. It looks Georgian to me – with crockery that I'm sure is also new from the last time we were here. But the real killer is hanging on the wall to my right: it's roughly six-feet by five, very glossy and dark. It's a photograph, by Hiroshi Sugimoto, of a seascape by night. To you and me, it's a six-foot by five-foot dark patch on the wall, but to those who know, it says that this man, Matt Finkelstein, has two hundred thousand dollars to spend on a museum piece of modern photographic art. Since it is completely black, I wonder for a moment if Matt could have sat in a dark cupboard with a camera with the flash disconnected and taken it himself, then got it blown up, but I don't think he has the nerve. If you study these things close up, you can see the wave patterns and starlight in the darkness. Obviously I can't acknowledge its existence by studying it, but he can't take the chance that someone won't. So it must be the real thing.

Damn him! He's got his retaliation in first: he's done all this stuff before the bonus. How could he? I'm sure he doesn't make that much more than I do, and Gloria is High Maintenance in a way that makes Wendy look modest. The only thing I can think of is debt – he must have mortgaged himself up to the eyeballs, and he's counting on the bonus as his lifeline. I smile and find myself reluctantly compelled to pay him the same compliment that Gloria paid to Wendy when she saw her jewellery: I ignore everything and sit down, pretending not to notice.

Today I saw a dead rat on the pavement. Now, if you're tempted to say, 'So what?', let me make clear that this is quite unusual for Sloane Square. I'm sure there are rats all over London, in fact there are probably as many rats as people, living off the rubbish that piles up on the pavements, surviving in the sewers and the gutters and rarely seeing the light of day. But this one had chosen to come out of the sewers and die, here on the pavement outside my flat, for me to find just as I'm leaving to go to work.

In case you're wondering, I'm not superstitious, but it did put me in a really negative frame of mind. I wondered if it could somehow be a metaphor for my life, and that made me think about God. Not the Money God, you understand, but the other one – the one I don't really believe in except for social occasions like weddings and christenings. If there were a Real One – just speaking hypothetically, of course – and He were looking down on this ant-heap of a City, scrutinising us, what would He make of us? Would He think we were actually doing any good with our one unrepeatable lives, making a difference to our fellow man, or would He view us simply as parasites, an irrelevance that could be wiped out with a giant aerosol spray, leaving the planet a cleaner and happier place?

You can guess where I came out, as I sat on the Underground and tried to focus on my newspaper. I found myself wondering if there was anything I'd ever done that was worthwhile, not in the sense of generating fees for the firm, but in the sense of making the world a better place. Like Bob Geldof. He was a rock star, and by and large I think rock stars are pretty worthless people – though it has to be said that the big names do make real money. But Geldof was different. He tried to make a difference, not just to his own immediate

circle, but to the whole world. Would I ever do that, spinning madly like a hamster in a wheel on this crazy money-go-round? And if not, should I be worried about it? Would I one day look back and say it was all worthless?

Well, not if I made two million this year. Two million would still not be real money, but it could make a difference. With two million – which after tax and assuming half the balance is held back in deferred shares or options is really only six hundred thousand – I could buy a proper place in the country – obviously with a second mortgage, because six hundred by itself doesn't get you there, but who cares about debt? Sensible leverage is, well… sensible. With two million, I could buy the kind of place where Wendy and I could invite houseguests for the weekend, possibly with our own shoot, and still get the 911 and the extras I was thinking about for the flat. Though on reflection the extras for the flat have less appeal now that Matt Finkelstein's beaten me to it.

By the time I reached Monument station I was feeling a lot better – forget rats, think bonus.

Thursday, 28th October –
B minus 49

Today Rory was happy. The sun shone and we were all smiling as we sat at our workstations and contemplated our good fortune. Truly, we work for the best of all possible bosses at the best of all possible firms.

Just kidding.

Rory called a departmental meeting. We were all a little nervous as we filed in to the large conference room at the end of the trading floor. We didn't show it, of course – except by the fact of all the joking and light-hearted banter going back and forth. Anyone observing us would have thought we were on something.

When Rory cleared his throat, you could have heard a pin drop. I was staring at the conference table, wondering what the hell was going on. You see, this was not our regular weekly bullshit session, where we take it in turns to try to claim credit for anything that's gone well, distance ourselves from anything loss-making and position ourselves as busy, productive, irreplaceable members of the team. This was a special meeting, called in the middle of the trading day, at theoretically one of our busiest, most productive times, and at this time of year you only do that for one reason: the bonus. I could feel sweat underneath my shirt and wondered if I should have put my jacket on, but that would have been too conspicuous. Anyway, I could see others were sweating too.

'Thank you all for coming.' I could have punched his ugly mug. As if we had a choice. At this time of year, if your boss asks you to stand on your head and sing Yankee Doodle, you ask in what key. 'I have some important news concerning compensation.'

That got our attention. I felt as if I could hear the entire room breathing – all thirty of us. The beating of my heart, my own pulse sounding in my ears, someone's stomach rumbling a few places down the table – everything became surreal for an awful, agonising moment. Let it be good news, dear God, please. Of course it wasn't good news – it couldn't be. It was all part of the softening up process.

Rory waved some papers, which none of the rest of us could see. For all I knew they were blank, just a theatrical prop to help get the message across. 'The department…' He paused, looking around the room. 'The department is thirty per cent behind budget.' A further dramatic pause. 'That can mean only one thing.'

One thing? It could mean several. It could mean Rory had failed to deliver what he promised management, and had decided to do the honourable thing –

fall on his sword and resign. His share of the bonus pool would then be divided among his subordinates, whom he so outrageously misled with his misguided strategy, and for which he insisted on taking sole responsibility. No – this is investment banking, after all. It could mean he wanted a presentation prepared, to which we could all contribute, on a fully democratic basis, to explain to management that the budget was never realistic, but merely a ploy to get him paid more last year, and that it should therefore be revised down to a more achievable level. No – he'd never admit to mere human fallibility. Most likely, it meant we were going to tighten our belts, fire some juniors, and have our expectations managed downwards.

'This means we are going to have to tighten our belts.' Bingo! 'We need to get control of our costs. With immediate effect, First Class travel will be restricted to members of the Executive Management Committee only.' Around this particular table, that means him. 'Travel to the airport will no longer be by taxi or limousine, but by public transport, excepting those employees whose terms of employment specify their means of transport.' Him again – a chauffeur's included in his contract. 'Overnight subsistence rates will be cut, and the list of approved hotels reviewed for those employees who do not have line responsibility for costs. In other words, if you're not liable to carry the can directly with management for costs incurred, you will be obliged to make economies.' He's the only one with that responsibility in this room, so I suppose he can work out for himself which hotels he'll stay in and whether he really needs the Presidential Suite. 'This is going to be tough on us all.' No, it's not. You're exempt. It'll be tough on the rest of us. 'But we have to keep our costs under rigorous control. I will also be reviewing the staffing requirements of our various business activities in terms of junior support.' True leadership – be decisive, fire some juniors, just before the bonus. 'And it goes without saying that compensation prospects for all of us are less rosy than they would have been had we actually delivered on what we all signed up to.' Now steady on – none of us came up with that budget. That was yours. We just get to pick up the tab.

We all nodded our heads in agreement. Then came a flash of inspiration.

'Rory, we're with you on this all the way.' I could see heads turning in my direction, envious scowls distorting their features. 'Not only will we focus on costs – we'll focus on revenues too! We need to really go for it this side of Christmas, show management that we can deliver and that we really are the best team in the City of London!'

I can see I've pissed off everyone in the room, except Rory, who's nodding sceptically in my direction, but then beams at us all and agrees vigorously, causing others to do the same. Soon the whole room is full of nodding, smiling, happy faces, as we all agree with the wisdom and intelligence of our Beloved Leader.

Did I tell you Rory has five homes? Yes, just the five. He has a five-storey house in Belgravia, with four staff, not counting his chauffeur, who's paid for by the bank. Then he has his 'place in the country', in Sussex, which I've already told you about. He has a chalet in Verbier, which as far as I can tell he never visits, and only has two staff; a villa near Antibes (four staff – he tries to spend most summers there, leaving early on a Friday afternoon and coming back on Monday mornings when he can't actually take a whole week off), and finally an apartment in New York (two staff), overlooking Central Park, in preference to the suite at the Four Seasons that he always used to take when he went on business. Someone said the firm might even be paying for his place in New York as part of his contract. Anyway, that makes five homes and seventeen staff, not counting the driver. He's a one-man employment machine, providing jobs and opportunities for so many people, his contribution to third-world development alone must make him a dead cert for a place in heaven.

By my calculations – based only on rumour and speculation – Rory must have been paid over twenty million pounds since he joined the firm four years ago. But do you think it makes him happy, all that material wealth? You bet it does. It makes him as happy as a pig in shit.

Wouldn't it make you happy?

Things are hotting up. I was sitting in my usual cubicle in the gents, reading a copy of the *Sun* left there by one of the traders, when I overheard a whispered conversation between two colleagues.

First voice (sounds American, I'm not sure who it is): 'Jackie's suing!'

This must be Jackie Thornton, a Vice President who was once considered a rising star, but seems to have had a bad year.

Second voice (Bill Mackay, who sits at the next but one workstation to me): 'Is that right? But do you think it's true?'

'Nah – but right now she's desperate. All she has to do is threaten to sue and she becomes ironclad. Not only can she not be fired – assuming anyone other than juniors will get fired – but she has to be well paid.'

'But the guy she's accusing is gay – she must know, surely? Everyone else does. He's the last person who would ever touch her.'

I almost start laughing at this point. They must be talking about Nick Hargreaves, who as far as I know is the only gay member of the team, and incidentally one of the top producers. The idea of Jackie, who thinks she's so smart, suing the only gay member of the team for what must be sexual harassment just makes me want to laugh out loud. But naturally I don't, because getting caught eavesdropping in the gents' is definitely not good form.

Talking of sexual harassment, the head of the Paris office was in town today, lobbying Rory ahead of the bonus. I've always liked Jean-Luc. He has the widest smile you ever saw, struts like a cockerel in a three-piece suit with a gold pocket watch, exuding a total confidence that he is the handsomest, coolest, smartest man ever to walk the planet (even though he's overweight and has a shiny bald head and glasses with inch-thick lenses). Only a Frenchman could do this.

Naturally, as he was on expenses, a few of us went out with him after work to catch up on developments in the French market, exchange views on business strategy, compare notes about marketing and origination, and get laid.

Did I say 'get laid'? I thought I did.

I suppose I owe you an explanation. One of the things about the pressure cooker environment of investment banking is that you need to let off steam. People do that in various ways – drink, drugs, gambling, you name it. In Jean-Luc's case – being a Frenchman – it's women. He's a member of a very exclusive club, called Andrea's, just off Dean Street in Soho. We piled into a cab and headed off there.

At Andrea's – where I am not a member – you ring the bell (naturally, there's no sign outside), wait while they scrutinise you on camera, then get buzzed in and go downstairs to be checked in by giant doormen, who are very respectful, and call you 'sir' and 'gentlemen', but everyone knows who's really in charge. Then you go through to a pretty mediocre, dimly lit bar, and pay nearly a grand a bottle for fairly average champagne, which you drink in discreet booths, designed to prevent you catching the eye of the other patrons. Just in case you know them.

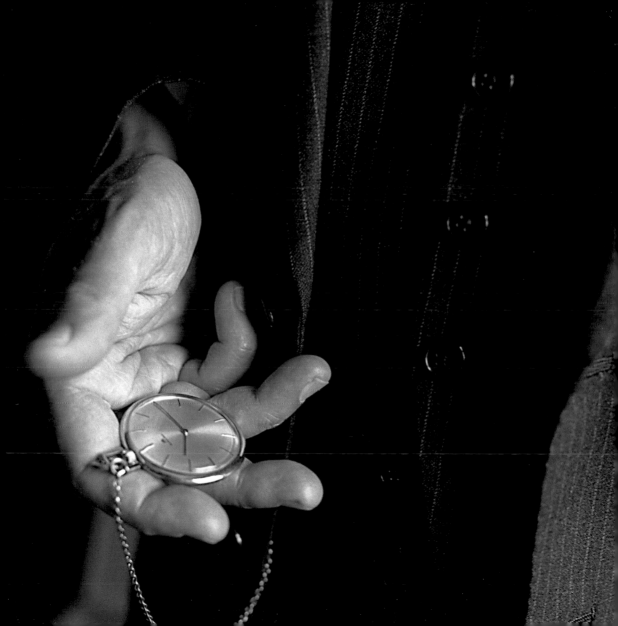

Sounds awful, doesn't it? Well, it is awful, until you 'go outside'. 'Going outside' is shorthand for leaving the bar to visit the other part of the club, where the girls are (and if you're so inclined, guys too). Of course, being married, I've only ever heard stories of what happens when you 'go outside'. It usually takes Jean-Luc about half an hour, which is not long, and afterwards he just wants to smoke cigarettes and stare wistfully into the fireplace. If he's in a particularly expansive mood – or wants to get you on side for something, like putting in a good word for him ahead of the bonus – he might invite you to 'go outside' too – on his expense account, of course.

Naturally, as a happily married man, I've never been outside.

There is a story that when Jean-Luc first joined the firm, he was taken to Andrea's by one of the old directors, long since departed in some bear market cull, who went outside to find a girl for his guest. When he brought her into the bar to point her in the direction of Jean-Luc, suggesting to her what she might want to do to him, she giggled, 'Oh, you mean Jean-Luc? I already know what he likes. We all do.'

I did say he was a Frenchman.

Which brings me on neatly to the Kai Tak Convention. If you've never heard of it, I'm not surprised, because it doesn't exist, at least outside of investment banking circles. The Kai Tak Convention is the unspoken code whereby investment bankers on business trips never, ever reveal on their return anything that might – hypothetically speaking, of course – have occurred in the course of their trip. Because that wouldn't be in anyone's interest, would it?

It's rather like the old joke about the patient in the dentist's chair. Just as the dentist is about to start wielding a particularly nasty looking drill, the patient's hand shoots out and takes hold of the dentist's testicles, gently but firmly, whereupon he looks the dentist carefully in the eye, and says, 'We're not going to hurt each other, are we?' Well, investment bankers don't hurt each other either. At least not when it comes to little things like minor peccadilloes on business trips to Hong Kong, Manila, Bangkok, Moscow, St Petersburg, New York, Milan, Paris, Amsterdam, Stockholm, Helsinki, Berlin, Prague, Madrid…

Anyway, without being crude about it, we get to earn a lot of Air Miles. It's one of the compensations of the job.

So there we were, sitting in Andrea's, drinking champagne, with sensual delights by the roomful just the other side of the wall, and what did we do? We talked about the bonus. You know a man is serious about something when he isn't distracted even by the pleasures that one of London's top clubs allegedly has to offer. Dedication is the name of the game – at this time of year, we all stay faithful to our purpose.

Anyway, that's all you need to know.

TUESDAY, 2ND NOVEMBER –
B minus 44

After last night, I feel rough. I look at myself in the mirror. It's one of those awful self-awareness moments. I can deal with the lines and the bags under my bloodshot eyes, the shadows and the first grey hairs. I can deal with my paunch, and the way I seem to be perpetually stooping after years spent hunched over a workstation. Those are almost a badge of office. What I can't deal with is the fact that I'm a loser. I hate my job. I hate my boss. But my biggest fear is that I'll get fired. Am I fucked up or what?

Don't answer that – I had a late night and now I'm feeling terrible, so give me a break.

And besides, there's something else. Last night the dream thing happened again. Rory was running through a forest in the moonlight, the ground covered in snow, working hard so that his frozen breath puffed out in front of him and desperate to escape, but I was faster. I was wearing an ice-hockey mask, overalls and carrying a chainsaw, which roared every time I squeezed the trigger, making him panic, blubber and run all the harder, though he knew and I knew that in the end he couldn't escape. What happened next is... well, you can probably guess what happened next. Wendy shook me, I was soaked in sweat, the sheets were drenched, and I actually looked at my hands to see if they were covered in blood and bits of gore from where I'd first sliced his arms and legs off and cut open his torso. My hands were actually shaking. I looked at Wendy and wondered if I was really losing my marbles.

I sat for a while on the edge of the bed, and Wendy fetched me a glass of water, though she had to hold it to my lips to drink, because I was shaking so much. She looked at me. I could see the question in her eyes.

'Just a dream. A bad dream. I'll be all right in a minute.'

Wendy never questions me. We're a team. We're on life's great journey together, and where I go, she goes.

I couldn't sleep for the rest of the night, and I looked like shit when I arrived at work. Mercifully, when I looked around the team, I could see I wasn't alone. There were a lot of other pale faces and dark-shadowed eyes. It's the time of year. Nick Hargreaves was the worst. If what I'd overheard in the gents was correct, I could understand why. And then I spotted something. On his desk he had a copy of a Christie's catalogue for an upcoming auction – 'The Christie's Africa Sale'. I got up and asked if I could take a quick look at it, and there, on page seventeen, I saw the machete from my dream.

Now this really freaked me out. This was weird. I mean, in the movies, yes, stuff like this can happen – but not in real life. Or maybe I'd seen a poster somewhere advertising the sale. Maybe somewhere in my subconscious I'd registered something without realising it. I looked at the date of the auction: three days before the bonus announcement. Weird.

♦ ♦ ♦

There are times when I wish I was Rory. That may sound strange, but it's true. I happened to be passing his office late this afternoon, when I heard his secretary confirming a business trip for him. Naturally, his chauffeur would pick him up from home to take him to – Biggin Hill! I suppose the name doesn't mean very much to you. It's a former Second World War airfield, you might vaguely recall it from watching old movies.

In investment banking circles, it means a whole lot more. In investment banking circles, Biggin Hill has real resonance. It means freedom – freedom from the burden of travelling with the general public on ordinary flights from airports crowded with ordinary people. To us, it means seniority, privilege and success. Biggin Hill means smokers.

Smokers? Let me tell you. A smoker is a private jet, and Rory gets to fly in a GV. You don't know what a 'gee five' is? I'll explain. The Gulfstream Five is not just any old executive jet. On the team we call it Air Force One. Rory once flew between four continents in twenty-four hours, changing flight crews as he went, juggling the kind of schedule that only global investment bankers can manage. The GV can technically take up to fifteen people, but Rory's jet is equipped just to take him and up to five colleagues. It goes at Mach .885, and flies at up to 51,000 feet, higher and faster than commercial airliners – public transport – literally leaving them in its wake. The firm doesn't own it. That might look bad to shareholders. We lease it. So not only does it make Rory's life more efficient, but it's tax-efficient too. And it's very efficient indeed when he wants to get away for a long weekend to relax and reflect on the future direction of the business, in Rhodes or Capri or Monte Carlo, maybe with his wife, maybe without. I'm sure if it was properly costed, we'd realise how much we save by providing Rory with the GV – it's a bargain and if anyone were ever to ask me – not that anyone would – I'd tell them I'm all in favour of Rory having whatever jet he wants. Or anything else, for that matter, at least this side of the bonus.

Though, in strictest confidence, there is one thing that really pisses me off. I've never been aboard the GV. No, not even once. Jackie has. In fact when she first joined, she and Rory used it for a whole load of strategy weekends and off-sites. But these days it looks as if she's grounded, the same as the rest of us.

Sometimes I feel as if I'm destined to live my life with my nose pressed against the window, a permanent outsider desperately peering in at where the real action is.

'He'll be flying alone, and he'd like the same stewardess as last time.' His secretary's words say it all – this man has arrived. 'No, he prefers the '85 Dom Perignon.'

What can I say?

Which brings me to the subject of expenses. In the good old days, it was understood that senior investment bankers didn't really need to worry about expenses – the market was roaring away, share prices were rising, we were all making money, and expenses were a detail. We actually used to authorise each other's expenses. An extremely workable arrangement. Today things are different – we live in a tougher climate. Accountants and financial controllers actually have influence, and management listens to them. They have the authority to question things like the two thousand pound bottle of Yquem I ordered at dinner with the Chief Executive and Chairman of Pattison Construction a few weeks ago. The total bill for dinner for four was a little over five thousand, which would not be unreasonable as part of the softening up process of an important client about to award us a major mandate. The irritating thing is that neither of them was actually present at the dinner – yes, I admit, it was one of those dinners, but God knows, we are all guilty of a little exaggeration now and then. Anyway, had they been at the dinner, it would have been a great opportunity to broaden and deepen our relationship. Instead, I took Wendy and her parents to dinner, and must have accidentally used the corporate credit card instead of my own. We've all done it from time to time.

The problem now is how to explain. And the worst part of it is that the person I have to explain to is an underpaid, uncouth, unpleasant individual named Samuelson, who thinks people like me are overpaid, arrogant, unreliable and probably dishonest. He's sent me a note, asking me to justify the expenditure, and copied it to Rory. If I ever find myself in a position of authority, little shits like Samuelson will be toast. Then a light goes on in my head. I have the solution.

I prepare two replies. The first is to Samuelson, apparently copied to Rory. I grovel and schmooze and weasel my way around the issue, saying that the chairman of Pattison Construction chose the dessert wine, and that there were four of them on their side, not three, as originally suggested (I just had a salad, instead of a main course), and pointing out that in fact three thousand pounds (thereby excluding the cost of the Yquem, which I had been obliged to buy out of courtesy for the client) for dinner for five people, of whom four were clients, was expensive, but not totally unreasonable, and had to be seen in the context of the development of the overall relationship, and imminent business prospects which I was not at liberty to reveal to him for reasons of confidentiality relating to price sensitive information. Just the right mix of taking him seriously, flattering him, sharing hints of 'inner circle' information with him, apparently treating him as an equal, but then reminding him who generates the revenue around here. And I apparently copied it to Rory, who would also see that I was taking him seriously, which could do his bonus prospects no harm at all. But then my masterstroke – I prepared a second version of the note to Samuelson, which I would actually copy to Rory alone. It was much brusquer, sharper, reminding him of the importance of carefully targeted, well thought through 'rifle shot' entertainment of the right people in the right way, emphasising the false economy of entertaining key clients on the cheap, and citing a ten million dollar revenue-generating transaction which we are very close to, but which is still highly competitive. To Rory, this is a reminder that I'm out there playing in the big league, swinging through the corporate jungle with the big hitters, there's a large deal just around the corner, and I'm not taking any shit from bean counters. When Samuelson fails to challenge me – which he would in a second if he saw this version – Rory will realise who gets respect around here. A masterstroke.

Afterwards, I worry that I've never actually met the Chief Executive and Chairman of Pattison Construction – I only know the Finance Director. But I guess that's a detail.

WEDNESDAY, 3RD NOVEMBER –
B minus 43

Today my worst nightmare happened. Well, not quite my worst nightmare, but something pretty bad. I got stuck on the Underground. To anyone accustomed to travelling by Tube, this may not sound too frightening – irritating, yes, even inconvenient, but not life-threatening. And for anyone used to living in the Third World country that modern Britain has very nearly become – at least outside the Square Mile – it was almost normal. Except that today we were launching a deal.

Today the European subsidiary of All Nippon Rubber were bidding for the Great Western Chassis Company. The bid would be announced at the market opening and I had to be there, so I left half an hour early to get into work. I

didn't actually have anything to do with the bid, and had never met the client, but it was essential to be around when the deal happened.

It was actually Nick who was working on the deal, having been briefed by the Corporate Finance team, and I had only learned about it last thing yesterday. But that really didn't matter. If it was well received, I'd make a point of going around to anyone senior and influential to tell them about the deal, so that they first heard about our role in it from me. I could bask in reflected glory, while Nick was still too busy actually doing the deal to take any laps of honour himself. On the other hand, if it went badly, I'd keep my head down and carefully pick my moment to wander over to anyone who was around from the Management Committee. Shaking my head sorrowfully, I'd let them know that it really was Nick's baby, and maybe he'd been just that little bit too ambitious, just a tad too aggressive, perhaps a little impatient – all great qualities in an investment banker, providing they weren't taken too far. He always had the best of motives, of course, and naturally he'd learn from this one and I for one was still optimistic about his long-term potential...

So that was the plan, but half way into work, midway between stations, the train stopped. To begin with, I wasn't concerned. I glanced at my watch, then carried on reading my paper. The carriage was crowded, but I had a seat and I wasn't sitting next to anyone too objectionable. After a few minutes, people started to complain. An old lady standing in the middle of the carriage, barely able to reach the straps hanging from the ceiling, started giving me 'meaningful' looks, as if she thought I was going to offer her my seat. Instead I just gave her one of my wide, beaming smiles, nodded encouragingly and went back to the FT market report. Still nothing happened, and then a very large, very pregnant, very ugly woman pushed her way through to me and asked in a thick Midlands accent if I'd mind giving her my seat. She was probably in her early thirties, but looked older. Her bushy, unplucked eyebrows very nearly met in the middle, she had a teenage boy's moustache, a mole on her cheek with long bristly hairs coming out of it, a sweaty sheen across her face and was wearing crimplene and polyester with clumpy, square, practical shoes. Why on earth would anyone ever breed from her? I looked around indignantly, but all the other seated passengers seemed to be very old, very infirm, and mostly women. Damn – this is what happens when you have a means of transport without First Class.

'Que?' I look at her, putting on a puzzled look, doing my best dumb Spaniard impression.

'You're reading an English newspaper.' She says it as if she's talking to a moron. Her accent doesn't help. Shit. I'm never at my best in the morning.

'Be a gentleman – can't you see the poor soul's expecting?' It's the old bag who was staring at me earlier, the one who tried to exert moral pressure on me. Some judge of character she turned out to be. The problem now is that having started out by pretending to be Spanish, but reading an English newspaper, I have to decide whether to keep up the pretence that I'm Spanish – which I can't, because I don't actually speak it – or admit that I'm English and offer her my seat. Just as I've decided to do neither, and ignore the lot of them and carry on reading my paper, there's a big jolt, and the train moves forward. The problem is, the pregnant woman, who would not be the lightest or slimmest I've ever come across, even without being pregnant, stumbles and falls onto the floor of the carriage, crying out in pain. As the train lurches forward in jumps and starts, everyone stares at me accusingly, as if I'm somehow responsible.

'Oh, for fuck's sake,' I sigh, and fold my newspaper and prepare reluctantly to get up and offer her my seat, when an older man steps forward through the crowd and kneels beside her, comforting her, trying to stop her idiot sobbing – I can see she's cut her knee on something, and it's bleeding quite badly – and then shouts across to the people nearest to the door, 'Pull the communication cord. She needs to get it seen to.'

I glance down quickly to check she hasn't bled on my shoes or suit. I'm wearing shoes by Lobb of St James's and my suit is hand-tailored at Gieves and

Hawkes. A close shave. As he turns back to her, he also gives me a hostile stare. What is it with these people? Am I expected to take responsibility for everything?

The cord is pulled just as we pull into the next station – Westminster – and the train stops, but the doors don't open, while station staff go up and down the platform looking for the source of the trouble. I check my watch. 'Jesus Christ – I'm going to be late.'

Now they're all staring at me.

'We're launching a deal.' I emphasise the word 'deal', in case they really can't get it into their dumb, bovine skulls that there are some things in life that rank ahead of a blubbering woman with a cut knee. Eventually some station staff open the carriage door and come to help her out. I breathe a sigh of relief, check my watch again, and calculate that I might still just make it, but then one of them asks if anyone saw what happened, and the old bag points to me and says, 'He pushed her.'

Can you believe that? This wicked, evil, malicious old bag accuses me – quite wrongly – of an act no gentleman would ever dream of. And they all stare at me again, and no-one intervenes to put her right.

'That's nonsense. I never touched her.' I almost add, 'I wouldn't touch her', but luckily I stop myself.

'Yes, he did.' She sticks her jaw out stubbornly, with one of those 'I will not be budged' looks that old people who are really long past their sell-by date sometimes put on. You just know there's no reasoning with her, and I have an almost irresistible urge to punch her.

The other passengers get out of the way as two of the station staff – young men in uniforms, who don't earn a bean compared to me, but infuriatingly take authority in absurd situations – ask me to get off while they call a police officer to establish exactly what happened. I look around helplessly, but no-one is willing to meet my glance and I have no choice but to get off the train, inwardly raging, and wait while a policeman is called to question first me, then the old bag. The policeman – when he eventually arrives – looks like a child. I wouldn't even hire him as a graduate trainee, but I have to listen respectfully and go through the motions of taking the whole situation seriously, all the time glancing at my watch and realising that the deal will be launching any minute. The 'victim' – who could potentially sue me if they believe the old bag! – has been taken to hospital for stitches, so she can't corroborate anything, but then the old bag relents and says she may be mistaken, and after leaving my contact details I'm finally allowed to go. Can you believe all this? I could kill her. It takes forty minutes – forty minutes of precious, irreplaceable deal time.

Inevitably, there is now a delay. The next train will be along in fifteen minutes. As I climb the steps from the station to try to hail a cab outside, I look back and glare at her. She deserves to die. I actually thought we lived in a free country run according to principles of decency and fair play. How naïve am I?

By the time I get to the bank, Nick's deal has been announced, everyone's smiling, high fives all round, and he's a hero. The shares did rise unexpectedly just ahead of the announcement, which is odd, but otherwise it was flawless. Nick grins at me.

'Where were you?'

'Oh – I… er… I was detained… I mean – held up. Well done, Nick. Congratulations.'

Damn. The only thing worse than a colleague having a deal go wrong is a colleague having one go well – and getting to claim the credit for it.

I'm on my way to New York for a day and a half of business meetings, sitting in the Heathrow Express, which I've discovered is actually convenient, quite comfortable and really fast, though of course that's not the point. I should have been collected from the flat by a limo service. Even if it takes longer, and costs more, it's a question of doing – and being seen to do – the right thing.

As I catch sight of my reflection in the window, I ask myself again if I'm looking at a loser. On the surface, everything looks fine: the steely grey eyes, the wavy brown hair, the dashing good looks that captured Wendy's heart almost ten years ago. But I can't escape reality. I'm thirty-seven years old, a Managing Director who has no-one reporting to him. I share a secretary, I have to request the support of members of the graduate trainee pool if I need help on something, and I'm not even properly paid. Last year I got a useless, insulting, mediocre six-fifty, before tax, and half the balance was paid in options that are so far away from being meaningful that I feel like papering the bathroom with them. Surely life has to be about more than this? Three years ago, on the back of a monster year in a raging bull market, I got nine hundred. A lousy, hopeless, useless nine hundred in what was otherwise a fabulous year. How am I meant to live? How am I meant to support my wife and child? Wendy has aspirations – it's only natural. And so do I. I don't think it's anything to be ashamed of – I want the best for myself and my family. We all do. That's why we're prepared to make the sacrifices we do.

And talking of sacrifices, here I am, travelling on the Heathrow Express, to board a BA flight where I'll sit in Business Class, not even at the front of the plane in First. There was a time when we used to joke about not knowing how to board a plane and turn right, but these days we're made to travel with the masses. Personally I think it's a bad business decision. The fact is that investment bankers ought to feel good about themselves. This is necessary in order to project an image of confidence and success, to reassure clients and win business. It's not as if we don't work hard – tell me how many other people you know who work the hours we do, who travel as much as we do, who ruin weekends as consistently as we do – and for what? It's clear I'm not even going to make a lousy million this year.

I stare out the window, too depressed for words. I need that million. It's not for myself, it's for Wendy and Samantha. In fact I really need two million. Fat chance. And all the time I have this nagging doubt that Rory doesn't like me. Yesterday he walked past the desk, stopped to exchange a few words with Nick Hargreaves, then chatted to a couple of the juniors, but when he passed my workstation and I looked up and smiled in a confident, relaxed way, he walked straight past, into his office, and closed the door! He didn't even glance at me. What is it – have I turned invisible all of a sudden? Am I totally transparent? And it's not the first time. Last week something similar happened by the coffee machine at the end of the trading floor. Rory doesn't use the coffee machine, because his PA brings him proper filter coffee from a machine in the corner of her office, so it was quite unusual to see him chatting to some of the guys, and I hurried over to get a refill. I smiled and nodded and said, 'How's it going?', just as he turned to go. I looked around, but he didn't even acknowledge me. What am I supposed to make of that? It can't have been an oversight – he cut me stone dead. Don't try telling me he had things on his mind, because we all have things on our mind at this time of year. It just doesn't make sense, unless… well anyway, it doesn't make sense.

You may find this surprising, but bonus time can bring out the worst in people. Sitting on the plane, sipping my first glass of champagne – before you ask, no,

it's not vintage, what do you expect in Business Class, sitting with the oiks? – I remember a Swiss German on our team a few years ago, called Richard Fresser. He pronounced Richard as if it was 'Rick–hart', but it made no difference, because we all just called him Dick. And that's what he was, three years ago, when Rory called him into his office to pay him. Dick felt the amount was so small as to be insulting, and he did a very Swiss Germanic sort of thing – he got up and stormed out of Rory's office, back to his workstation, where he swept the entire contents onto the floor, and then walked out, shouting Swiss Germanic insults in the direction of Rory's office. Only a Swiss German would act like this over money – talk about a provincial, small-minded, little prick. The rest of us would have been much smarter. The next day, he realised that even the insultingly small amount he had been paid would never reach his bank account if he was no longer an employee of the bank in a month's time, when the cash actually got distributed. So he tried to come back in. Can you imagine? Naturally, Rory's PA had immediately cancelled his staff entry pass to the building and his corporate credit card and had cut off his company mobile phone. So when the security guards called from reception to ask if he could be allowed up, we all went downstairs for a laugh. The best part of all was that he never really saw the funny side. It must be a Swiss German thing.

We're an hour away from landing at JFK, and I haven't slept a wink, though the lights have been turned down and the rest of the passengers in Business Class seem to be sound asleep. There's a very attractive stewardess, who keeps fussing around me, asking if there's anything else she can do for me. Her name badge says she's Donatella, which I suppose is Spanish or Italian, and she has a slightly dark complexion, which I don't usually go for – being a gentleman, I prefer blondes. But I've worked my way through most of a bottle of champagne, and I'm finally starting to relax, so that I can appreciate the way the top buttons of her blouse are undone and the tilt of her head and all the eye contact. I look at her and wonder what she would say if I offered her dinner in Manhattan. She looks interested and I'm the only passenger still awake in Business, so we could potentially… And afterwards, naturally I'd stand her up. I stare at her and ponder the possibilities.

Have you ever had sex on an aeroplane? I thought not. It's actually not that great, especially in Business – or so I've heard. In First, where you have seats that fold flat, turning into beds with small wooden partitions around them, the girl can slide in under your blanket and you can quietly, unobtrusively get on with it – at least that's what I've been told. In Business, forget it. You have to use the toilet cubicle, which is not only unbearably cramped, but by this stage of the flight isn't exactly fragrant.

Did I ever tell you about Piers Hawkins? Piers was an Englishman with the 'right' connections who worked on our team for a couple of years and then joined a German firm. The reason he moved – the real reason – was that no-one on the team took him seriously after an episode on a flight to Hong Kong. It seems he made out with a stewardess in the toilets, when he thought everyone else was asleep. But the first time they did it, they made too much noise, banging up against the door and the partition wall, and woke a few people up. That would have been okay if they had discreetly exited, one at a time, and called it a day. But after a pause and a change of position, they started again, and a few more people woke up. By this stage, things were pretty tricky, but they might still have got away without too much embarrassment. But then – and at this point I have to give him full credit – he had another go. Yes, that's right – jet-lag be damned, they really went for it. This time they woke up everyone, and when they finally emerged, the cabin lights were on, everyone was staring at them, and they got a round of applause.

Naturally, no-one took him seriously after that, particularly his soon to be ex-wife.

Which brings me to the question of infidelity. No, not infidelity to Rory – that would be unthinkable, at least this side of the bonus. I mean good old-fashioned fooling around. Looking at Donatella, who has quite an athletic figure, I could imagine having a really good time with her – briefly. Should I be concerned that Wendy would be upset if I did this? Well, yes, technically she would be upset, if she knew. And if she ever played away, I'd kill her. But is there really anything morally wrong about the brief enjoyment of purely physical pleasure by a man without any emotional commitment or betrayal? Some of the team say that it's no worse than the physical, sensual pleasure you get from an old-fashioned shave in a barber's shop, or a really invigorating massage: the person you're with is faceless, unknown to you before or afterwards, simply providing a service. It just happens that in this case, the part of the body that gets serviced is… well you know the parts that get serviced. It's all a question of relative values. In some cultures it's perfectly normal and widely accepted, and if anyone should be able to stand above the constraints and the relative norms of everyday morality in one particular society, surely it must be global investment bankers who benefit from a truly international perspective. We really are different from the rest of you, so there can't be any moral problem. Can there?

I'm glad we settled that. But the real question is, do I need the complications now, when I'm utterly stressed out about the bonus? I'm not even sure I could perform right now, so – nah, I won't bother. Not this time. I look away from Donatella, close my eyes and pretend to go to sleep. By the way, you remember the terms of the Kai Tak Convention, don't you? I only shared this with you because we're on an aeroplane. I'm a happily married man, after all.

I'm a bad traveller. My first morning in New York, I always wake up ridiculously early. It doesn't matter, because I call Wendy, tell her it's 5:00 am and I'm already up rehearsing for my first presentation of the day. It never fails to impress her, though today she's in a hurry to get me off the line because she's running late and she's trying to squeeze in a session with her personal trainer before she goes to have her hair done. Anyway, New York is a great town, and I love to press the switch that pulls back the drapes – electrically operated, of course, to give me a perfect view of Manhattan. Then I order room service, so I can feast on eggs benedict while I enjoy my first blow-job of the day. And then my second and my third – perfect bliss with no interruptions.

Did I say blow-job? Damn. Well, yes, actually I've switched on the pay TV so I can get myself in the mood for what might come later. Shit. I said 'later', didn't I? I told you I'm not that sharp in the morning. I meant to say 'when I get home to Wendy'. I'm a married man, after all, and I'm here on business.

It's the weekend. Saturday morning, I'm mildly jet-lagged after my exhausting trip to New York, and there are only forty-nine shopping days to Christmas. Samantha's nanny has weekends off, and Wendy claimed to be worn out by all the sleepless nights I've been giving her – did you get that: I've been giving her! –

so I had to go and get Samantha when she woke up and give her breakfast. It's not my fault that Wendy's so shattered. Her personal trainer gave her a couple of really hard workouts while I was away. She said he really stretched her. I'm starting to resent him. I think he's the reason I'm up early on a Saturday morning, seeing to Samantha. Can you believe I have to do this? Now's the time I could use some juniors: pour her muesli and her juice, make sure she finishes, wash her face, brush her teeth, get her dressed. I'm a Managing Director of a major investment bank, and still I have to do this stuff!

Of course I love her dearly. I always wanted a perfect, little blonde just like her mother. She looks so cute in the back of the Range Rover, wearing her Ralph Lauren dungarees and Baby Armani roll-neck sweater. But first thing in the morning she's… well, I would have said a drag, but how can anyone you love so much ever be a drag?

Later, when we're all ready, we go shopping for Christmas presents. Now, this is a challenge. How much should I spend? If it turns out to be a good bonus, I'm happy to be extravagant on the present front. But if not, well it might still make sense to be generous, though generosity born of guilt about failure is not true generosity. It's a way of concealing inadequacy. It's a way of diverting attention from the real issue: Daddy, you're not a real man because you didn't even make a million. Little Mickie's Dad made two million…

We take a cab to Harrods, and I go mad in the toy department, leaving Samantha with Wendy while I organise almost three grand's worth of toys for delivery: every Barbie they have, a full set of Sylvanian families, a hand-made wooden doll's house, you name it, my little girl can have it – because I love her and I want her to have the best. Well the most, anyway.

Today I went to church. Well, when I say I went to church, what I really mean is that I walked past the church, went fifty yards down the road, heard the organ playing and a hymn being sung, turned around and went back, to peer inside. You can probably guess my views on religion. I had my fill of compulsory church services at boarding school. It's not that I mind how people choose to spend their Sunday mornings, but it has to be said that traditional religious belief sits uncomfortably alongside the life of the global investment banker. We serve markets, rather than gods. Or perhaps the markets are our gods. Anyway, truly efficient markets are morally neutral, and our role, as the people who service those markets, facilitating global trade and economic development – the very foundations of our civilisation – is to be completely unaffected, some would say indifferent, in the face of the choices we have to make between different courses of action. If we have to recommend a choice between a strategic restructuring of a huge conglomerate, resulting in massive job losses, or an enormous investment programme, leading to huge job creation, the moral and social consequences of any decision have to be put rigorously aside. We have to focus purely on the financial and economic results of any eventual decision. Which one carries the biggest fees?

That brings me back to church. I pulled the heavy oak door open and peered inside. There was a typical Chelsea crowd, singing in a desultory fashion, off-duty management consultants, lawyers, journalists, a television presenter whom I vaguely recognised, plus assorted spouses and children. What were they doing here? It was Sunday morning, the time when some of us have only just surfaced, unshaven, to venture out and buy a paper, and here they were, scrubbed, shaved, dressed, and worst of all, actually smiling. It was as if they'd all been given monster bonuses, and didn't have to worry any more. But I knew – and in their hearts they had to know too – that they were running away from reality. Whatever they got from church wouldn't buy them a 911 Turbo Cabriolet, or His and Hers Rolexes, or even a week in Barbados at Sandy Lane (the only place to be seen there). I shrugged. Losers. I closed the door, quietly, making sure not to disturb them and wandered on to the newsagents, feeling hard-nosed and aggressive, my mind in overdrive again as I started working through bonus scenarios and how I'd spend the money. As we say in investment banking circles – he who dies with the most toys wins.

MONDAY, 8TH NOVEMBER –
B minus 38

The Monday morning meeting. It's amazing how everyone at this time of year suddenly discovers enormous prospects for new deals, new clients, new business, just around the corner, conveniently after the bonus gets paid. There is a view, to which only a cynic would subscribe, that the bonus is not really paid for past performance during the year at all, but for your perceived productivity going forward, particularly in the next financial year. That's why if you can, you put off really big ticket deals until late in the bonus year, so they're fresh in everyone's memory when those key meetings of the Executive Compensation Committee take place. Like I said, a dollar earned early in the year isn't necessarily wasted, but it doesn't carry as much weight as a dollar earned the week before the Compensation Committee meets.

So today we all sit around and see if we can out-bullshit each other as far as exaggerated claims go. Rory sits and looks bored, until Jackie's turn. She smiles at him, flutters her eyelashes, and starts into a classic line that we've all heard a thousand times before.

'I'm working on some major prospects in the Middle East. It seems the Sand People really want to re-structure some of their portfolios in the light of…'

'Who?' Rory's voice cuts right across her. We all look up to see what's going on. Surely Rory isn't going to object to the old chestnut of enormous Arab wealth, huge trades, vast oil riches that need recycling – we've all used it. But he's leaning forward in his chair and staring intently at her, like a predator stalking its prey, about to spring. She looks flustered and blushes as we all gawp at her.

'The… I meant to say, the Arabs.'

'Do not – I repeat – do not use racist terms again.' Aha – now I see what's going on. 'It's unacceptable in this firm, or, I suspect, in any other. I will be taking appropriate disciplinary steps.'

Well, how about that? I look down the table for Nick Hargreaves, who's grinning. An ambush! It was a fucking ambush. She didn't know it, but Rory was waiting for the chance to nail her. Sitting there at the end of the table like a nodding dog, he was waiting for her to take one step out of line – and she did. He's playing a pretty aggressive game here, though he has a roomful of witnesses on his side, and at bonus time we'll make sworn statements to anything he wants. If the rumours are right, she's got a formal complaint in hand against Nick, which most people know can't be true, but she's done it to strengthen her own position ahead of the bonus round. But Rory, bless his little cotton socks, has decided to take her on. Why would he do that? He couldn't care less if Nick gets hung out to dry. But on the other hand, it might reflect badly on him, as the head of department, if sexual harassment can go on right under his nose. So he must be… yes, that's it. He must be planning to turn it around, to put her in the spotlight, maybe even suggesting she's homophobic as well as racist, and turning the tables on her. In theory, according to the firm's Diversity Code, we must never make any kind of comments, jokes or allusions which run up against the '–isms': racism, sexism, ageism, you name it, we can't do it. Except that Jackie just did. And so today, Jackie my girl, today the Big Beast of our particular Jungle has decided you're going to be lunch.

Jackie goes deathly pale, stares at the table and nods in acquiescence.

THURSDAY, 11TH NOVEMBER –
B minus 35

Jackie left today. Or at least, she didn't show up for work, and later I heard that a letter had come from her lawyers. It looks as if Rory's in fighting mood, and we've all been told we may be called upon to give evidence. Hell, right now I'd give evidence that she was guilty of cannibalism if it got me paid. Yes sir, your honour, I saw her with my own eyes. She lured passing children in off the street, offering them sweets as bribes, and after that, well I hesitate to explain in polite company what I witnessed with my own eyes… but all of it's true, I swear… at least until after the bonus.

The sad fact is that it won't make much difference. I've no idea exactly how much she was paid last year, but my guess is not much more than two fifty, which wouldn't make much difference, whether it was split evenly thirty ways across the whole department or just seven ways among the Managing Directors (which it won't be: I'm sure if Rory's going to this much trouble, he'll keep it for himself).

She didn't even have many decent clients for us to fight over. In fact she had one or two very difficult and badly paying clients that most of us would want to avoid. Maybe that was why she left. Anyway, she was here less than three years, and now she's history. Let's think no more about her, and instead think about… the bonus! On the way into work this morning I did some more scenario planning. I started with three million, but stopped when I realised just how ridiculous that was. Or put it another way: if I get three million, I won't have a problem thinking what to do with it.

So instead I thought about some of the worse case scenarios – a bit reluctantly, I admit, in case thinking about them made them more likely to happen. It's not that I'm superstitious, you understand, but you never know. Anyway, I started with six fifty, the same as last year. That was disastrous. As I've already explained, six fifty gross means three ninety net, and that in turn means less than two hundred in folding money – which is a catastrophe. Take off the overdraft, the 911, and Barbados, and that's it… it's all gone… an entire year of my life… and for what?

Then I went further. I started thinking about five hundred. At five hundred (three hundred after tax, one fifty in real money), I couldn't even pay off the overdraft, once I'd bought the 911 and paid for our winter holiday.

I shouldn't have done it to myself – God knows, my life is stressful enough already – but I then ran through four hundred, two fifty and one hundred. Each was more surreal than the last, each more terrifying as I worked through the consequences. At anything below two fifty I might as well not bother to get paid. Could it really happen? Was I really just torturing myself unnecessarily? I thought I knew the answer, but then I passed Rory in the corridor, and he didn't even glance in my direction – again. I felt like grabbing him by the shoulders and shaking him. Does he know the effect he has on people?

Tonight I got home and Wendy wanted to make love. We don't usually make love at all during the bonus season, not because it might be bad luck, but because it's impossible to concentrate when this huge uncertainty is hanging over you. Can you imagine having sex with your beautiful, expensive, wonderful, expensive, loving, expensive, adoring, expensive wife while all the time you're wondering whether you'll make a million, half a million, two-fifty, or just a useless, hopeless, utterly disastrous hundred thousand?

Anyway, I walked in the door and looked into the dining room. I could hear music. The table was set and candles were lit. For a moment I almost freaked – were we expecting guests? No – the table was set for two. And when I wandered through to the kitchen, there was no Samantha – she'd been put to bed early. And Wendy – well, Wendy looked terrific. She was wearing a low-cut, simple black gown by Armani, high-heeled stilettos from Fratelli Rossetti, a white gold necklace from Tiffany and amazing diamond and pearl earrings by Kiki McDonough. She looked complete, the way my wife should. And when she came and kissed me, with one of those lingering lips-half-open kisses, I thought… well, I thought what if I make two million? Think what I could buy her then. Now that is true love.

Anyway, she took my hand and guided it to her thigh, so I could feel what she was wearing underneath her gown. I probably haven't mentioned this before, but I'm a sucker for lingerie. Okay, all right – I admit it – not lingerie, just stockings, preferably black, with suspenders. And no panties. Now I'm blushing, because I've told you too much, but what the hell – when I say stockings and suspenders, I naturally mean La Perla, and no, when you buy one of these outfits, you don't get change from a hundred pounds. So if you don't know what I'm talking about when I say how much I appreciate this stuff – I understand.

Wendy had prepared a simple supper that started with beluga caviar, beautifully presented on crystal dishes filled with ice. It was followed by smoked salmon and a superb Grand Cru Chablis that I'd never heard of, but was delicious and which she must have picked up during the day to surprise me.

And afterwards, well you can probably guess what happened afterwards. She whispered in my ear, told me how she knew it was always tough on me at this time of year, and led me into the bedroom…

As if…!

What actually happened when I got home was Wendy in tears, because the useless, hopeless, ugly, hairy-armpited Bulgarian shot-putter we employ as a nanny had stomped out after a row when Wendy caught her stealing again. It's not that we're materialistic, it's just a simple matter of principle. Another pair of ear-rings had gone missing, and some cash that was left lying around, and a few odd CD's, and then Wendy saw her late in the afternoon going through her handbag, and that was it. You can guess the rest – Wendy had the full hell of the late afternoon and early evening and no-one to help her. First the trauma of bathing Samantha at the most difficult time of day, when she's at her most awkward, putting her pyjamas on, reading her bedtime story, getting her to sleep, obviously having to cancel the session she had booked with her personal trainer, so that just when she most needs help to de-stress, she maxes out on STRESS. Anyway, I walked in and she was on her third gin and tonic. To be honest I can't blame her. Not that that stopped me. I work damned hard and I don't expect to come home to a wife who's half-cut, hasn't even thought about my supper and just unloads a whole bunch of trivia when the whole time I'm in a huge panic about the only matter of substance in our lives right now – the bonus.

I slept in the guest bedroom.

Dinner at Colon, the new 'in-place' on the King's Road. This was something of a coup, because it's only just opened, and it's really hot. Apparently Hugh Grant's a regular, and someone told me Madonna and Guy have been there. The reviews say the food's mediocre, the service slow, the surroundings 'airport-lounge' bland, and the prices outrageous, but that's not the point, is it? When I called to make the booking, they said there were no free tables, even on a Monday night. This really pissed me off. The maitre d's at these places think they're so fucking important because they have power. They have the power to allow the rest of us to feel good about ourselves, which is absurd, because they don't get paid a bean and mostly they're seriously inadequate people who have to get off on jerking real people around – people like me. Anyway, I had a moment of inspiration, and called back a few minutes later, putting on a different accent, and tried to book a table in Rory's name – and it worked. The idiot who took the booking even said how much he was looking forward to seeing me again. Rory has a permanent inside track to all the hottest places. Don't ask me how he does it, but he does – only tonight, he was renting it out to me!

Sometimes, I try to dissect Rory's life, to work out how he does what he does and still succeeds as a global investment banker. Not that I'm envious, you understand, or somehow left in the shade, but sometimes I do wonder. Did I tell you he went to breakfast with the Prince of Wales? It was a breakfast for business leaders. Obviously nothing concrete or specific came of it, and no-one was expecting anything to come of it, but it was a great event to be invited to – it sent a signal, it said that some people had arrived, and others hadn't. Clearly, I hadn't. And then he was invited to a garden party at the Palace. How did that happen? Who puts the invitation lists together? Do they go around the various firms, filling slots with senior people? No – because generally speaking, investment bankers hardly ever get invited – I can't imagine why. So what is Rory's inside track? And how does he juggle all this social stuff and still play the role of investment banker? And it's not as if he's just any investment banker – he's the Leader of the Pack.

It really fucks me off.

But tonight at least, I was briefly a hero… well, at least in Wendy's eyes. I called her from the office to tell her where we were having dinner, and she was over the moon – it went some way towards healing the rift after last night. But then she had to hang up, which irritated me, because her personal trainer was coming to the flat to give her a massage.

Anyway, we were having dinner with the Harrises. He works for Schleppenheim, the US investment bank that made its name in the arbitrage business. They're aggressive as hell, towards each other as well as the competition, and this time of year is sheer murder for him. By halfway through the evening, I was actually starting to feel sorry for him. It's good to get a sense of perspective now and then, which you can only do if you meet someone really unfortunate. Last year he made a million and a half, but that's not the point. He's seriously overweight, drinks like a fish – though only after hours – looks pale and pasty-faced, and I'd rate him a serious health risk. When I look across the table at him, I see myself in a worst case scenario in, say, ten years or so – except Bob Harris is two years younger than I am. He's thirty-five years old and looks like an unhealthy fifty-year-old. He has bad skin, eczema, and dandruff. He's rich as Croesus, but I know he'll never enjoy it. I really like being with him.

His wife is called Trish, they were childhood sweethearts, and I suppose she doesn't notice how overweight he is, or his bad skin or dandruff. She's plain, dumpy, has no idea how to dress, and has come out tonight wearing a two-piece suit that could have come from M & S. How can she do this to him? I can tell Wendy really likes coming out with her too.

Conversation centres on – guess what? – the bonus. Schleppenheim have had a terrible year. They placed a couple of big bets early on, using the firm's own capital, and both went terribly wrong. They went through a huge upheaval, even fired some of their management, which shows just how bad it was, and haven't recovered since. Naturally, no-one feels sorry for them – those who live by the sword…

He shovels his food into his mouth as if he's worried someone will take it away from him. Maybe they do that at Schleppenheim. These US firms can be really aggressive. And he drinks like a fish, slurping great gulps of Chassagne Montrachet as if it was beer. Between courses he smokes – filthy French cigarettes that I know will make our clothes smell horrible, and which cause other diners to complain. But somehow I enjoy seeing him do this to himself. Thank God Colon hasn't succumbed to the tyranny of the health Nazis and still allows smoking.

The thing about dinner with Bob and Sally Harris is that I always come away feeling good about myself, and terrific about Wendy. Compared to Bob Harris, I'm Brad Pitt. And Wendy – well, Wendy's Jennifer Anniston. For once, even the money doesn't matter, because these guys are just rich losers. They've stayed so true to their working class roots that they wouldn't know Giorgio Armani if he bit them on the arse – which he might, if he saw how they dress. I don't know what they do with their money, but they certainly don't spend it – at least not as far as I can tell. They don't even own a car. Can you believe that? Bob doesn't drive – he just never learned. They live in a big house in Balham – yes, Balham. They have four kids, and no nanny. That's right – no nanny. Someone even told me they have no cleaners or other help either. She does it all herself. Yes, really. Everything – the cooking, the cleaning, the school run, even the ironing. I heard they give away a huge amount of their money each year to charity, though you'd never know it – they don't say a word. Wendy and I do our bit too, of course – but we do it publicly, at charity auctions where we can show what we believe in by bidding for items donated by generous sponsors. Last year we spent five grand on a two week yacht charter in the Caribbean (actually worth ten if you paid the full retail price, but we did it for Pro-Motor, the motorists' lobbying group against bus lanes); we paid three grand for a week in a really plush ski chalet in Zermatt (actually worth four and a half, but I did it at a riot of a livery dinner for the Honourable Company of Stock Jobbers), and we picked up five cases of vintage port for four grand (worth at least half as much again, but we did it for the Poodle Sanctuary). We all do our bit for charity, but why not give it a competitive edge?

Anyway, back to the Harrises. I've noticed how he not only bolts down his food, but he always goes for the least healthy items on the menu too. I wonder if he has some kind of unconscious death wish, a desire to escape from his awful life, the sole Brit in a firm that epitomises American corporate aggression on steroids, a house in Balham with no help, and a fat wife who can't dress to save her life. No matter how much he gets paid, I always know that when we meet for dinner, Wendy and I will look like the stars, and the other diners will assume we're taking our poor cousins from the country to see the sights.

But tonight was different.

It pisses me off now just to think about it. It started to go wrong in the most horrific way imaginable. We'd just finished our main course, and Wendy and I were feeling good about refusing dessert, while Bob and Sally ordered crème brûlée, when I heard a familiar voice calling out from across the restaurant.

'What a surprise – fancy seeing you here.' It was Rory – Rory!!! He was sitting at a table on the far side of the restaurant, with a fantastically beautiful woman whom I thought I recognised, though I couldn't be sure. How could he actually be here, on the very night I'd booked a table in his name? What had

the maitre d' said when he arrived? Coincidence can stretch so far, but this was insane!

I beamed and got up as he came over, his hand outstretched and a warm smile on his face.

'Rory – it's great to see you.' I wiped my sweating palm down the side of my trousers and held out my hand in greeting as I prepared to introduce him to Wendy, Bob and Sally, all the time searching desperately for an excuse about why I'd used his name to book a table.

But he walked right past me. He walked right past me and shook Bob by the hand. Bob! Of all the people he could shake by the hand, it was this loser from Schleppenheim, this shabbily dressed, overweight, unhealthy guy with dandruff.

Bob didn't get up but kind of grunted and shook Rory's hand in the gruffest, most perfunctory manner possible.

At this point I had some catching up to do. 'I... I... er... didn't know you two knew each other.'

They ignored me. Rory started talking with huge enthusiasm about some charity that Bob was funding for asylum seekers. Asylum seekers! I mean – what on earth is going on – and Rory approves! Has he lost his marbles? Has Bob? Or have I?

They talk nineteen to the dozen for almost five minutes, with Sally joining in, while Wendy and I just look on, nonplussed, irrelevant and by-passed, until finally Rory says to Bob – yes, to Bob – 'I didn't know you knew these people.'

These people – he hadn't even said hello, let alone gone through the motions, which one would normally do, of being polite to an employee's spouse. He feels he can call Wendy and me 'these people'. We're fucking REAL PEOPLE, in case you didn't know it, and yes, I might have stepped mildly out of line by booking a table in your name, but it's not the worst crime in the world and right now our life is hell because of you and your fucking bonus.

Obviously I don't say this. I smile, Wendy smiles, Sally smiles, and Bob, whom I could kiss, says, 'We're really old friends – we go back a long way.'

'Really?' Rory seems genuinely impressed, and for the first time looks at me, a little perplexed. 'Let me introduce my wife.' He walks halfway back to his table, calls over, 'Darling, come over here for a moment, would you? There are some people I'd like you to meet.'

She smiles, a beautiful, dazzling, radiant smile and gets up to come over. She's wearing a dress by Dolce and Gabbana, shoes by Manolo Blahnik, she's carrying a Gucci handbag and wearing jewellery by Graff. Everything is top of the range – things you have to wait in line for, personally designed, with no compromise – if you need to ask the price, you needn't bother, and no queue jumping, no matter who you are or how big your wallet. At least a hundred grand is walking across the restaurant towards us, and the body is perfect. Toned, tanned, and above all, elegant. She moves across the room in an almost stately fashion, impervious to the looks and stares of every woman in the place not to mention every man. It must be my imagination, but it's as if a hush descends on the restaurant as she makes her way serenely towards us, oblivious to the effect she's having. I can feel that my tongue is hanging out – metaphorically, of course – and I want to take her clothes off there and then and… but then I turn and stare at Rory as he says, 'Bob and Sally, may I introduce my wife? Claire, darling, let me introduce you to two of the greatest philanthropists in the City of London.'

What? Did he really say that? Philanthropists? I want to shout 'Give me a break – you've just said he gives money to asylum seekers'. But of course I don't. After Bob and Sally have shaken hands with Claire, and Rory still hasn't introduced Wendy and me, I hold out my hand and say, 'Hi, I'm Dave Hart – I work with Rory.' I turn to Wendy and smile. 'And this is my wife, Wendy.'

Her eyes don't exactly glaze over, but it's as if somehow she doesn't quite see us.

'For me.' It's Rory. He's looking at his wife, and then at Bob and Sally. 'Dave works for me. Not with me.' He's speaking very quietly. I can feel myself blushing, stupidly, and I nod and grin. Can you believe that? I actually nod and grin. Am I a monkey or a nodding dog or what? And all for that fucking bonus, which isn't going to be any good anyway.

Wendy and I look on as awkward, sidelined teenagers while the grown-ups have a conversation, and when it's over, Rory and Claire return to their table and don't even say goodbye to us. Bob and Sally's crème brulées have arrived and they start spooning it in, looking fat and content as if nothing had happened. I sit and wonder guiltily if Rory knows I booked the table in his name or not. He might not – I could easily imagine him asking for a table for two and no mention at all even being made of my booking. On the other hand, if he does know, and worse yet if he was actually embarrassed, he'll wait for his moment. With the bonus just weeks away, it won't be long coming.

I want to scream.

TUESDAY, 16TH NOVEMBER –
B minus 30

Last night was bad. I was entering a large stately home, the sort you see in films about the great families of the eighteenth century nobility. There was ivy growing over the outside of the house and I used it to climb up to a balcony where the windows were open and I could enter a bedroom. There was a huge four-poster bed with drapes drawn closed around it. I was wearing black clothes, a mask like Zorro, and carrying a sword. I pulled the drapes back at the side of the bed, to reveal, lying naked before me – Claire! And then… then

I woke up, and Wendy went through the usual ritual: glass of water, arm around my shoulder, ignoring my sweat and my shaking hands and chattering teeth.

I was going to rape Claire.

There, I've said it. I was actually going to rape her, to repay Rory for the way he insulted not just me, but my wife as well. Our honour was to be restored by taking hers – and implicitly his as well. God – I shake my head and wonder how far all this will go, whether I'll ever get used to bonus time, whether I'll ever put all this behind me.

It's 2:00 am I can't get back to sleep, so I go into the kitchen, make a pot of tea and sit staring out of the window.

What's it all about? Is it just money? It's an awful question. I think I know the answer to that, so I make my thoughts go elsewhere. How much longer? I'm thirty-seven. How many more Christmases will be dominated by The Bonus? How much longer will it rule my life, validating my existence, determining my self-esteem? Should I be working on an escape tunnel, building a glider on the roof of the bank, to carry escapees away to freedom? But what is freedom and where would I go? I know almost nothing about anything worthwhile or – God forbid – useful. If Wendy tells me a cupboard door needs fixing, I tell her, 'So get a man in to do it.' But what is a man?

I reach, sadly and with an air of resignation, for the whisky. Not ordinary whisky, you understand: this is a special Macallan, a rare bottling from the Second World War, and not available for sale to the general public. I've always thought Macallan make the best, but this is the best – and the rarest – of the best. Every drop is irreplaceable, and as I sip it – with just a dash of water – I feel better about myself. How many people in London tonight are drinking whisky like this? Or in the country? Or the world? Not only can very few people afford it, but even fewer know of its existence. This is a truly rare malt. I doubt if even Rory has ever tasted it. It was bought as a gift to present to an

important client after a major deal, but somehow the celebration dinner kept getting postponed and finally never happened. I can't even recall how it found its way to my flat. Oh well. Needs must and all that. I take another sip and feel better. This is what it's all about.

Rory is looking at me, he's stopped ignoring me, but it's odd. I don't feel comfortable, almost as if he knows that last night I was going to rape his wife. He can't, obviously. Still, it's a little unsettling. I even find myself wondering if he can smell the whisky on my breath, and might ask whatever happened to the presentation bottle of Macallan ordered for the Chairman of WunderKorp.

I really can't decide whether it's better to be noticed, or not to be noticed. I know that sounds facile, but frankly speaking (NB: whenever an investment banker says 'frankly speaking', remember he's not speaking frankly – maybe I should have told you that sooner, though you've probably worked it out by now) – I think there's a higher risk profile involved in being noticed than not. Some would argue that at bonus time the best rewarded people are those regarded as uncontroversially good, high achieving, apolitical individuals whom everyone respects and nobody has strongly negative views on. Yes – really.

And then there's reality. You knew I was bullshitting just now. This happens when I haven't slept, I've been out to dinner the night before, and when I can't sleep during the night I hit the whisky. It's a stupid, ridiculous formula, and at thirty-seven I really ought to know better, but – well, you can guess the rest.

Let's talk about Rory. No, not about me – you know enough about me. Rory is forty-three years old. I know, he's just six years older than me, and I know what you're thinking. He read history and got a First. But then, he would, wouldn't he? I read history too, at Balliol College, Oxford, and got a Second. Rory was at Exeter. No, before you ask, Rory didn't go to Exeter College, Oxford. He went to Exeter, Exeter. Yes, that's right – the place in Devon where the yokels come from. And before that he went to a comprehensive school. Seems unthinkable? He was one of the beneficiaries of the broadening of the City's catchment area after Big Bang. It should never have happened. They wanted to go fishing in a bigger talent pool, where they wouldn't be limited to people like me, but could instead hire people like… him. Don't ask me why. The result is that he's part of the City's nouveaux riches, the new generation of high achievers who've made it without showing any respect at all for the finer traditions of the Square Mile. I'm a third generation stockbroker, a man with his roots in the City. My father was a liveryman like his father before him, a member of the Honourable Company of Stockjobbers and Brokers, and ended his career as the partner in charge of settlements at Carruthers and Stroud, before it was acquired after Big Bang, and my grandfather was a private client stockbroker at the same firm. As an only child it should have meant that I was set up for life, but somehow it never happened that way. Grandfather was a drinker and a womaniser, and he spent his money. At least my father didn't drink, but he did get through his too. I last saw him three years ago, when he brought his latest wife to see Samantha, his first and only grandchild. I forget her name – Susie or Floosie or something. She was younger than me, so I made a point of asking if she minded me calling her Mum.

I haven't seen them since.

Anyway, this isn't about me. Rory's always been a Golden Boy. Youngest ever member of the Executive Committee. Hoping to be the youngest ever Main Board Director. Some say he's Sir Oliver's heir apparent. He's certainly heading for the top. A fast track with a rocket up his arse. Me, on the other hand… but this isn't about me.

He has two children – apparently. I say that not because I doubt they exist, but because I don't see how someone as perfect as Claire could ever have had children. Unless she's immune to all the things that affect other women – or buys her way out of them. The really irritating thing is that she seemed not only beautiful, elegant, lively, adoring and bright, but a nice person as well – at least if you were part of her universe, which Wendy and I evidently were not.

In this business, it's easy to forget what a nice person is. Elsewhere, I'm sure you see them all the time: nurses, for instance, or teachers, firemen, ambulance crews, even social workers. I bet they're all nice people. Or most of them, anyway. But investment bankers? You must be kidding. We eat nice for breakfast.

So what does Rory think of me? You might wonder whether he doesn't see me as just another faceless, brown-nosing, unprincipled whore, who'll do anything for money. Would you like to sleep with my wife, Rory? Sure – go ahead, why not? You pay our bonus, after all. Humiliate me, stop me sleeping, give me ulcers, high blood pressure, a heart condition. Why the hell not? I'm yours, Rory, yours for the duration. So go ahead – abuse me, the way you kick a puppy and it comes back, nervous, frightened and ingratiating, always wanting more.

Except you wouldn't treat a puppy like this.

Monday, 22nd November –
B minus 24

An amazing thing happened tonight. I'd waited until Rory finally left the office, around eight, before packing up my things to go. The rest of the team were doing the same, once someone had checked that the coast was clear, and I went down to the main entrance to walk towards Bank underground station. It was dark and pouring with rain, and for some stupid reason I'd left my umbrella in the office, so I was splashing through the puddles when a car horn sounded behind me. I turned around and saw a dark grey Bentley flashing its headlights. Rory's car! It pulled up beside me, the rear window slid down and Rory peered out at me and said, 'Get in.'

For a split second, an impulse of pure madness almost overcame me and I found myself thinking how fast I could run to get away, whether I'd make it to Bank underground station before the car could catch me.

But of course I smiled meekly and got in.

'How are you?'

My jaw dropped. As if he could care. Actually Rory, I'm going out of my mind worrying about what I'm going to be paid in three weeks' time – as you know only too well, you bastard. In fact you probably have the numbers right there in your briefcase.

'Great,' I smile back confidently.

Rory nods to the driver, who slides the big car smoothly back into the traffic, muscling his way elegantly into the correct lane and heading for the Embankment, which is vaguely in the right direction for me, although Rory hasn't actually bothered to ask where I'm going.

'Good.' He stares out of the window.

'It's a filthy night. Thanks for picking me up.'

He ignores me and the silence stretches out. I look at the Bloomberg screen in the back of the car, the walnut desk top that folds down from the back of the front seat for him to place his laptop, so he can work on the way home, and the walnut cabinet where he keeps his whisky. I could use a glass right now, though of course I don't say anything. The Bentley's a slightly stretched version, so there's plenty of leg room, and the seats feel like armchairs. This is definitely the way to travel.

'Where did you first meet Bob?'

'Bob?' I'm genuinely puzzled.

'Bob Harris.' He glances at me, irritated, as if he thinks I'm playing a game.

'Oh, sorry – well, Bob and I go back a long way.'

'How far?'

'We were at university together.'

'Really?' He turns and looks at me again. 'Weren't you at…?'

'Balliol.' I say it almost guiltily, weighed down with the shame of the privileged under-achiever.

'That's right. Did Bob go there?' He seems slightly incredulous, his eyebrows raised as if it's somehow inconceivable that someone as clever and successful and different from the rest of us as Bob Harris could have gone to Oxford.

'Yes.' I can't help a note of petulance creeping in.

'What did he get?'

I pause and look away. 'I'm not certain – he was a couple of years younger than me. But I… I think it was a First.' Actually, I know it was a First, but who cares what class of degree people get anyway? It really doesn't say much about the sort of person you are.

Rory just nods. 'Do you think he'd come and work for us?'

Now I'm startled. 'Bob? Work for us?'

'That's what I said.'

'But… what would he do? Do you mean actually work on our team?'

'That's right.'

'But, it's not his field. He does arbitrage.'

'He could learn.' Rory turns and looks at me again, with what I think – hope – is a twinkle in his eye. 'We could break him in doing your job.'

I try to laugh, but it comes out as a sort of half-strangled gurgle, and I'm

almost sure I catch the eye of the chauffeur in the rear-view mirror, sneering at me.

'Don't worry.' Rory slaps me on the thigh – yes, he actually slaps my thigh! We've just driven down the sliproad onto the Embankment and Rory leans forward to tap the driver on the shoulder. He pulls over to the side and stops, while Rory turns back to his laptop and starts tapping into it. I realise it's my cue to get out, and open the door.

'Goodnight.'

Rory ignores me, and I could swear the driver's grinning. I close the door and pull my collar up to protect myself from the rain. It's a damp, dark night, the nearest tube station is ten minutes' walk, and there isn't a cab in sight. Did he do this deliberately? Is he really thinking of hiring Bob? And if he is, surely he doesn't think he'd take my job? Bob's a heavy-hitter. No heavy-hitter would ever want my job.

Would he?

WEDNESDAY, 24TH NOVEMBER –
B minus 22

There are rumours abroad.

I know that rumours are worthless, empty, unreal garbage that aren't worth the paper they aren't printed on. But it's twenty-two days till the bonus – twenty-two fucking days – each of them twenty-four hours long, with sixty minutes in every hour and sixty seconds in every minute, and those of us who have to live through each one of those seconds, wondering, speculating, enduring the uncertainty, need something to keep us going.

There are three principal rumours. The first, which no-one believes, is being spread from Paris by Jean-Luc, who claims to have heard that Rory is planning a team move to an American firm. Team moves were flavour of the month a few years ago when the market was booming and the Germans and the Swiss were hoovering up talent like it was going out of fashion – until of course it did go out of fashion, they dropped a bundle, and now we have to sit tight and wait while the market naturally corrects itself, the indigestion works through the system, and the next wave of dumb money comes along. But the Americans aren't dumb. Greedy, sharp-elbowed, vicious, single-minded and utterly ruthless, yes – but they're not dumb. And anyway Rory and most of the team would hate working for an American firm – if you think we have a tough time, you have no idea what an American firm does to its people. So this first rumour, that Something Is Happening on the team, is bullshit. Because if something were happening, I'd know about it. Wouldn't I?

The second rumour, which is only slightly less implausible, is that the entire bonus is going to be waived, because the firm as a whole is barely profitable (thanks partly to fixed income trading, and partly to private equity, neither of which has anything to do with our area, though that wouldn't necessarily matter). The idea of the entire bonus being waived for the entire firm is ludicrous – even in the worst bear market, which this is not, you still get paid something. This rumour probably comes from management, and is more softening up to make us feel pathetically grateful for whatever scraps eventually come our way. Do they think we're stupid, or what?

It's the third rumour that intrigues me. Someone on the team has been insider dealing – using confidential client information to make a killing in the stockmarket. My first instinct is to dismiss it. Who on our team would ever break the law? Well, on reflection I suppose it would depend what was at stake. Would I break the law for a million? No, probably not – at least, not unless it was a dead cert that I'd get away with it. You wouldn't either, would you? Would you? To take a real risk, I'd need to make real money – five million upwards, and I'm your man. Oh, come on – don't be so shocked, not after what you thought just now. I look around the desk and wonder who it could be – and how it is that the rumour has started. You actually have to be quite brave to break the law, and I don't see any heroes on our team. Has someone confided in someone else, perhaps after they had a drink too many? I can only gaze around and wonder.

The good thing is that this takes my mind off my latest dream. Did I tell you about the latest one? It happened last night, and it was Claire – again. I'd tied Rory to a chair, bound and gagged, but not blindfolded, so he could see what was happening. I'd tied her to the bed, the big four-poster, naked and frightened, her wrists and ankles bound with silk, while he watched, powerless to intervene. I straddled her, naked myself save for a black leather mask, her master, her dominator, all-powerful – until my fucking dick went limp. Can you believe it? I think it was Rory, sitting there bound and gagged, but still in control. His eyes said all he needed to say: have her if you will, but I'm still the one who'll pay you.

Or not. And actually thinking about it, I went limp. Just like that – in a matter of seconds I went from a strutting master to a servile wimp. But then, with Rory's evil eye on me, it's hardly surprising, is it?

FRIDAY, 26TH NOVEMBER –
B minus 20

Today at work I did the headhunter trick. It backfired terribly.

You've never heard of the headhunter trick? Well, it goes like this. I pretend to have a call on my line. I get up and turn away from the rest of the team, as if seeking privacy, and as I do so I hit the 'Privacy' button on the dealerboard that stops other people picking up my line or listening in to the call. This usually acts like a beacon to attract everyone's attention. It generally means either a row with the wife, a call from a lover, trouble with the bank manager, or a headhunter. Now, you can go into a private conference room at the edge of the trading floor, where everyone can see you talking through the glass walls, but most people prefer to try to be inconspicuous by hiding themselves in the general buzz of the desk.

So I stand there, talking quietly to myself, saying, 'Sure… How much?… Guaranteed for how long?… Sure… you've got my home number?…Okay. I can't talk right now… Okay, bye.'

And do you know what happened next? Nick Hargreaves – yes, Nick, the gay guy I felt so sorry for – gets up, grinning at me, and walks over to Rory's office. He closes the door and sits with Rory, and points out at me. Yes, he fucking points at me! And Rory looks up and nods – and laughs. I can't believe it. I can feel I'm going stupidly red, and I pick the phone up to call home – not that I need to phone home, but I need to be busy, and right now anyone will do.

And then it all gets worse, because a man answers, and I don't know who it is, and I realise I've dialled the wrong number. In my stupid anxiety I've dialled Rory, and now he puts me on the speakerphone, so he and Nick can hear me.

'Yes?' It's Rory's most superior, supercilious voice.

'Oh… er…' God help me, right now, please dear Lord, if I can only play one of my jokers now, let me do so. And then it comes to me. 'Rory, are you planning to visit Paris for the football? I only ask because Dominique Dupont was angling for an invitation, and he's given us a lot of business over the past twelve months. I'm going to be in Frankfurt, but if you were free, I'm sure he'd be flattered. Obviously I wouldn't ask you to go especially, but if it could be combined with one or two other visits, it might…'

'Definitely.' He interrupts me, and I can see Nick is nodding seriously now, the laughter wiped from his face. 'Put me down for it, and I'll arrange to see some other people as well.'

He clicks off the line and I close my eyes – Rory loves football. Thank you, God, I owe you one.

MONDAY, 29TH NOVEMBER –
B minus 17

Some bastard broke into my car. I couldn't believe it. Why do people do these things? The driver's window was smashed, so the alarm must have been going on and off all night. Lucky for us it was parked around the corner. They couldn't take the radio, which is built into the dashboard, but they ripped the front off the glove compartment, which was empty, and then they took the fire extinguisher, which I found lying, empty, in the gutter. And they scratched the side of the car, all the way along the side, and for what? What do they think they're doing? What are they actually achieving? They stole nothing, but caused hundreds, maybe thousands of pounds of damage. Who are these people? Who are these faceless, feral creatures who prey on the rest of us? I bet they don't have to scare themselves shitless worrying about the bonus. They just fuck things up for honest, law-abiding people who work hard and try to do their best. Wendy had to take a taxi for the school run – it was that or walk – and she was seething with anger. I called the garage to collect the car and get it taken in for repairs and respray, and the insurance company to see about getting the repairs authorised. By the time I'd dealt with that, I was twenty minutes late for work, and this is not the time of year to be late for work.

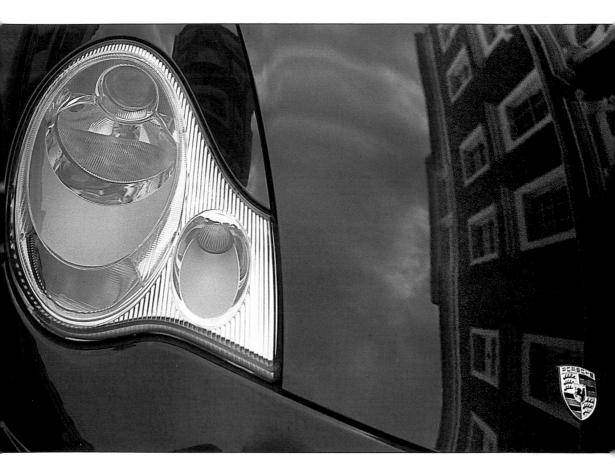

Bastards. I'd hang the lot of them, except that would be too quick.

Which brings me to justice. Not justice in the legal sense, but what might be termed appropriate compensation – people getting what's coming to them. I'm a great believer in the principle that what goes around comes around. I knew Rory by reputation some years ago when he was at Swiss Credit, who were our great competitors for a piece of business that my then boss, Harry Braithwaite, was after. I was very close to Harry, I'd been to his house for dinner many times, and he'd even agreed to come to our flat once for supper – at the time we lived in Kennington, so it was quite a commitment on his part. So we turned up for the beauty parade at the client's offices, and there was Rory, leading their team, sitting in the foyer when we arrived and trooped in with our presentations and handouts.

Rory set the tone at once. 'Oh, here come the coach party.'

Harry said nothing, but was obviously seething, and headed off to make some calls before we were summoned to present to the client's top management. The rest of our team were stony-faced, ignored Rory's remark, and sat down to wait.

I know you're going to ask, so let me tell you – I smiled at Rory's remark, made eye contact and nodded to him: as one professional to another. I'm not quite sure why I did this – he was a competitor, after all, and we needed to win the business. But anyway, we didn't, Rory did, and Harry was fired.

This was a source of great regret on the team, because Harry was the closest thing I've known in the City to a popular team leader. But popular, as they say, is for girls, and within days of Swiss Credit winning the business, Harry was gone.

And then his successor was appointed – an outside hire, there was a lot of buzz going around about the amazing package the firm had come up with, and suddenly the announcement: Rory was joining to head our team.

Naturally, on his first day in the office, we all went to see him, offering our observations on the rest of the team, trying to get the measure of him, putting ourselves forward as his obvious deputy and right hand.

And he didn't like me.

I can't say for sure that he disliked me, but when he looked at me, there was no respect, no warmth, none of the familiarity that had briefly existed between us for one tiny instant when he had insulted my boss – and, I suppose, my team and my firm, in fact technically myself too – and I had smiled and nodded to him. It was almost as if he didn't recognise that this wasn't reflex ingratiation with a powerful, senior figure from another firm, or subconscious arse-covering in case I ever wanted to apply to him for a job, or he became – as he now had – my boss, but instead the natural acknowledgement of one bright, quick-witted, high calibre individual by another.

So there's no justice now, but one day there will be. One day I'll have my moment in the sun. Because Rory should have acknowledged that we had history together, that we had connected before he even met the rest of the team, and that we were two of a kind. But he didn't then, and he hasn't since.

It's okay. I can wait. My time will come. You don't believe me? Just wait and see.

TUESDAY, 30TH NOVEMBER –
B minus 16

A lucky break. Rory noticed I was late yesterday, and called me in for a chat. Apparently the verdict on the team is that my acting was so good about the car being broken into that it couldn't possibly be true, and someone – probably that slimy sycophant Nick – had spoken to him.

He actually appeared solicitous, as if he cared. He asked me about Wendy – he called her Mandy – and what our plans were for Christmas, and how things were going, and I could tell he was looking me over, trying to work out if a loser like me really could take another firm in sufficiently for them actually to make me an offer.

Would it bother him to lose me? It's not as if I actually do much, but then none of us really does much, though the hours are long and the travel is punishing. But enough business always seems to come our way that when the markets are strong we can talk the board into paying us and covering our overhead and expenses and the whole great bandwagon keeps trundling on.

After that, I decided to take a lunch break. No, I didn't have a client lunch – not even one of those 'client lunches' that the firm pays for but the client never actually makes it to (usually because he hasn't been invited – hey, no-one's perfect!). No, this was an actual lunch break. The sort everyone is theoretically entitled to, but which our macho culture means that no-one actually takes. A sandwich and a bottle of juice at the workstation, because markets are moving and we're too essential, too committed, too serious about our work, to do anything as frivolous as taking a lunch break. It's just about acceptable to slip out for forty minutes to play squash or work out at the gym if the markets are quiet, but taking lunch is for cissies.

So I took lunch – God knows why, it was just a moment of madness brought on by stress and anxiety – and now Rory really was worried.

When I got back, he called me in again.

'I thought things were clear between us. What's going on?' This time he looked positively hostile. At least I thought it was positive, because it showed he was concerned. One way or another, I was on his radar screen, and payday was just around the corner.

I played it cool. Yes, idiot that I am, I actually played it cool. 'I just went out for lunch.'

This clearly perplexed him. 'And?'

'And that's it. I was grateful for our chat this morning, I know you've got my best interests at heart – that's it. It's an important time of year, and I trust you.'

'Ah.' He leant back in his chair and made a bridge out of his hands, resting his elbows on the arms of the chair and staring at me. 'I see.'

At this point I felt somewhat less cool and confident than I had a few moments earlier. I realised I might have overplayed my hand.

'So you've dealt.' He was really fixing me, looking for the slightest clue.

'D – dealt?' I had to cough to clear my throat. 'What do you mean?'

He gestured out to the trading floor. 'This doesn't matter any more. You'll wait to be paid, and then you'll be off. You've done a deal with another firm. You're leaving.'

I experienced an almost irresistible urge to be violently sick. I could feel myself blushing. This was a disaster – if Rory thought I was definitely going to leave, there would be no point paying me. That would be a catastrophe, compounded by the thought that 'my' money would go to some undeserving bastard like Nick Hargreaves. Imagine him spending my money, while I sat at my desk, watching as the days went by and I felt more and more naked and Rory and the whole team waited for me to resign – except I had no job to go to. I'd never be taken seriously again.

'Rory – I'm not leaving.' I tried to put on my firmest, most resolute voice. 'I'm not saying I haven't been tempted, or that there aren't other opportunities out there, but this works for me, and this is where I'm staying.'

Even as I said the words, I could see his expression change as he realised that now I might be telling the truth and he struggled not to laugh. And then it dawned on me. This time I'd really fucked myself. If he believed me, which he apparently did, he'd have no reason to pay me well at all – he'd concentrate his firepower on the people who might really leave.

'Thank you.' He said it with an almost syrupy sincerity. And yes, I believe that at that moment he was sincere, because I'd just saved him several hundred thousand pounds that he could use on someone else.

Oh, God – why me?

A funny thing happened today. I got in just about on time, feeling grim after yesterday, but determined not to be ground down by the everyday horror of my life. I'm a survivor, after all. In fact, that's a common trait among all investment bankers – we're all survivors. If there had been investment bankers on board the Titanic, everyone else might have drowned, but the investment bankers would have made it to the lifeboats. The women and children might somehow have been left behind – but not the investment bankers. The rescue ships would have arrived and found a few lifeboats and rafts containing... investment bankers. Because whatever happens, we never give up. It defines us. It determines who we are. And if anyone, ever, is inclined to dismiss us, to despise us for our unprincipled greed, or our egotistical superficiality, or the urgency and desperation of our lust for money and material possessions, all I say is this: could you do what we do?

Anyway, Nick left the Christie's catalogue on my desk. On my desk. I don't know why. He and I never discuss things like this – collecting antiques, buying at auction, personal things like that.

But there it was, and I flicked it open – and saw again the machete from my dream. It was only a few weeks ago, but it feels like a lifetime. I stared at it for an age, and when I looked up, I saw Rory looking at me from his office.

I slammed it shut, got up and went straight to the gents. When I got there I splashed water on my face and stared at myself in the mirror. This was freaky. Did he know? Could he have any idea about the dream? Did he have a sense that somehow our destinies might be linked?

No, he was probably just bored and wondered what I was reading when I should have been working. It took me a few minutes to compose myself before returning to the floor. When I did, I saw that Rory had a visitor. Sir Oliver was with him. I looked around at the team.

'What's Sir Oliver doing with Rory?'

Nick looked up from his workstation. 'Chairman's annual visit to the trading floor, I suppose. Came down to chat with the team, put names to faces, he said – given the time of year.'

'But – but, I wasn't…'

Nick smiled. Yes, he actually smiled. 'That's right – you weren't here. But I don't think he wanted to see you. He didn't say anything, anyway.'

Of course he wouldn't say anything – but I would have. I'd have told him how much business I'd done during the year, thrown in a few names of key clients, talked about the prospects for next year, how excited I was, the huge potential that's out there, just waiting to be had – and I missed my chance because I was in the gents'. In my mind's eye, I'm planting the machete from my dream in the middle of Nick's forehead, splitting his skull wide open and letting his brains spill out onto the floor.

But of course I smile. 'No problem. Maybe I'll catch him on the way out.'

'Maybe you will.'

After that I don't move from my seat, alert for any sign of Sir Oliver getting up to leave. And then, when he does leave, Rory gets up and walks out with him, the two of them with their heads down, engrossed in conversation, and Rory seems to steer him away from the desk, so that he leaves the trading floor by the far exit. In my mind's eye I play out the scene from that Arnold

Schwarzenegger movie when he pilots the Harrier jump-jet, coming up in the hover alongside a skyscraper full of terrorists and sweeping the whole floor with his cannons. Only this time I'm the pilot and I'm sweeping the trading floor, smashing workstations and glass-panelled meeting rooms and doing my best to lower the headcount this side of the bonus.

I look up and see Nick grinning at me.

I'm taking Wendy to the Barbican for a concert, and I have to go and collect her. It makes no sense, but she's tired and fraught and when she's in this mood it's no use arguing with her. Apparently she was due to see her personal trainer this afternoon, but at the last minute he cancelled her appointment because he had to see another client, and now she's pissed off. So I leave the City by underground, go home to change into my dinner suit and then drive her back towards the City in the Range Rover, intending to park at the Barbican. I wouldn't bother, but we're entertaining one of my more important clients and his wife.

Needless to say, the traffic is appalling. As I sit on the Embankment and fume, I curse Ken Livingstone and his useless congestion charge. What's a fiver, for God's sake? If you really want to keep poor people off the roads, make it a tenner or more. Or introduce special lanes for rich people who can either pay an extra charge or get their firms to pay it for them. That's the way they used to do it for the old Communist Party officials in Moscow. Why can't we do it properly and learn from people who really knew how to run a country – they never took any shit from their poor people.

When we get there, stressed out by the drive, we spot our guests, but we're running dangerously late if we're going to have a pre-concert drink. Our guests are the director of the London office of Nippon Heavy Rollers and his wife, Mister and Mrs Kanehara. They're an ill-matching pair. He's wearing what looks like a Moss Bros DJ that's two sizes too big for him, with an elasticated bow tie, which is positioned off-centre, but I daren't put it straight, because that would make him lose face, whereas she has an evening dress that looks like Catherine Walker and copious strings of pearls, possibly Mikimoto. She's small and cute and probably in her mid-thirties, whereas her husband is much older, maybe early fifties and a lifelong corporate man. I wonder what she's like in bed, and how much her husband makes – what would she say to a quick £10k?

Time is short, so after we apologise for being late, I shoulder my way through the crowd to the bar. I need to get a bottle of champagne, quickly, and get a few glasses down them as fast as possible. The Japanese are hopeless at holding their drink, so the sooner he's half cut the better.

As I push my way to the bar and shout my order, an old woman standing beside me hisses, 'Do you mind? I've been waiting here nearly ten minutes.' A funny thing happens at this point. It's as if my life is so full of shit that I have to take from all sorts of people, that to begin with, I just assume I have to take it from her as well. But then I do a sort of double-take as I realise that I've no reason whatsoever to be afraid of her: even at bonus time, she has nothing on me. I make a point of ostentatiously handing over a fifty pound note and telling the barman to keep the change as I pick up the ice bucket in one hand and four glasses, stems carefully intertwined between my fingers, in the other. Then I lean close to her and whisper in her ear, all the while smiling my usual friendly, engaging smile, 'Could I make a suggestion?'

'What?' She looks puzzled, as if I might have something genuinely useful to say.

'Why don't you go fuck yourself?' She tries to take a step backwards, but the crush around the bar is too great, and so she has to stay where she is, her face inches from mine as I continue my beaming smile. 'Just a suggestion – feel free to ignore it.'

I shrug and smile again as I shoulder my way back through the crowd. YES! Sometimes it's nice to bite back.

We down a few glasses, but then the bell sounds and we all rush in to take our seats. Within minutes I'm asleep and only wake up when Wendy nudges me because I've started snoring.

It's when the lights come up at the interval that I focus on the programme on my lap – it's open at the list of individual sponsors of the evening's performance, and there at the top of the list of Platinum Supporters is… Rory.

I close my eyes and take a deep breath, trying not to lose it altogether, as I imagine this all-knowing, ever-present being pursuing me during my every waking – and sleeping – hour. Wendy casts anxious glances in my direction, recognising the symptoms, and ushers our guests out to the bar.

When I emerge a few minutes later, my normal self-control restored, Wendy and the Kanehara's are talking to an old woman who seems vaguely familiar – it's the old bag from the bar. I'm about to duck behind a pillar when Wendy sees me and calls me over.

'Darling – come over and meet Lady Gore-Williams. Her husband is Sir Brian Gore-Williams, the governor of the Bank of England.'

Wendy is delighted. She obviously thinks she's Made a Useful Contact, someone with whom I can Network. Don't you just hate those pushy corporate wives at drinks parties who positively insist you meet their husband, because he's the director in charge of internet strategy at Amalgamated Lawnmowers, and who get pissed off when your eyes glaze over and you look over their shoulder for someone more interesting? Anyway, right now I look at the old woman, look at Wendy, look at the Kanehara's, and imagine spraying an Uzi sub machine-gun round the room, wasting everyone in sight, blazing away until the magazine is empty, peace descends and my last cartridge rolls across the floor amongst the bodies.

Lady Gore-Williams surprises everyone when she nods at me and smiles.

'Oh, we've already met. Your husband passed on some very useful advice to me, which I'm sure my husband will appreciate. Did you say your name was Hart? I must mention your advice to my husband – I do believe he's been invited to lunch with your chairman, Sir Oliver Barton, next week. He was saying to me only yesterday that he didn't think they have much to discuss, but I'm sure I can give him a tip or two.'

The great thing is, she says it all with the sweetest look of utter sincerity on her face – a harmless, lovable little old lady, as she slides a knife between my ribs and twists it sharply round and round. As my heart sinks further, and a horrible feeling of nausea threatens to loosen my bowels, I can't help thinking to myself, Christ, and I thought I was good – she's the one who should be an investment banker.

SATURDAY, 4TH DECEMBER –
B minus 12

Today I reached the Point of Maximum Desperation. Unlike PMT, PMD comes just once a year – but it's got to be much worse than a whole year's worth of PMT. It's the moment when I realise just how bad things could be if I don't get paid. Little things can spark it, passing a Porsche showroom or walking down Bond Street, but this year it was the credit card statement. We – by which I mainly mean Wendy – had spent eleven thousand pounds on the credit card in November.

Now, eleven thousand may not sound like much to you, but in certain poor countries whole families can live on that much for a year! I know this may seem ridiculous, but think about it from my perspective – on a basic salary of a hundred thousand, I simply cannot afford to run up credit card bills like that. So when I got home from the concert late last night and found the credit card statement with the mail on the drawing room table, I sat in an armchair and got utterly and completely depressed. I don't mean that I was feeling 'a little low', or 'less than a hundred per cent' – I was FUCKING DEPRESSED! A major league Blackie had descended on me, a whole pack of Churchill's black dogs, and they weren't letting go. As if symbolically, my special bottle of Macallan was empty, reflecting the state of my bank account and my bonus prospects going forward. Looking at it, I could swear it was the bloody Bulgarian shot-putter who finished it, probably as revenge after Wendy stupidly re-employed her, mainly out of desperation that the absence of childcare meant she had to stop her sessions with the personal trainer – apparently she needs his help to de-stress, because of all the pressure she goes through at this time of year.

Anyway, here I was, sitting in a million pound apartment in Sloane Square, a Managing Director of a major investment bank, days away from the annual bonus round, and I was broke. Wendy didn't make it any better by saying how much she'd saved – yes, saved! – by taking advantage of the fact that the sales start before Christmas these days and actually she had found some amazing bargains: a Donna Karan scarf at a thirty per cent discount, another handbag from Coach at a twenty-five per cent discount, and so many new shoes at amazing savings that I finally lost count. How many shoes can a woman wear? But they were all bargains. In fact she had saved us so much money that now we didn't have any left.

The more I thought about it, the more solutions I found. I could always raise the overdraft, get some more credit cards and extend our credit with the various store cards that Wendy uses. The main thing was to act with confidence. We live in a fickle, superficial world, which responds to us so often directly in proportion to our expectation of its response. Of course, I'm rich –

very rich, actually. I have investments, naturally, and offshore accounts. So I must be well off. And it must make sense to extend my credit. Otherwise I might take my custom elsewhere, and that would never do, would it? I thrust my jaw out and put on my grim-faced but determined look. I do grim-faced but determined very well. Eleven grand on the credit card was not going to be the straw that broke the camel's back. I was solvent and I had a good job. In fact compared to the vast majority of the population I was among the favoured few. It was important to remember that, to keep a sense of perspective that would allow me to bounce back. Have you noticed how I do that? No matter how bad things are, I always bounce back. I have something called resilience. Nothing ever defeats me. Push me over ten, twenty, fifty times and I always bounce back – another smiling investment banker propelled ever onwards in life by invincible self-belief. Phew.

TUESDAY, 7TH DECEMBER –
B minus 9

The Christmas party. It's strange having it just before the bonus. Normally it's timed to be a few days later, when most people can pretend to each other that they've been fantastically well paid and are happy, successful people, and any-one who can't hide his depression can get hopelessly plastered at the firm's expense.

Only this year was different. Rory sent around an e-mail announcing the date, the venue and most importantly the fact that because of cost-cutting measures, the MD's were picking up the tab instead of the firm. Yes, I said the fucking MD's were picking up the tab, and he hadn't even consulted us. Can you believe that? By now I suppose you can. But the other surprise was the venue. It was going to take place in the staff canteen!

I'd always known there was a staff canteen somewhere in the basement, but I'd never actually been there. It was a place where support staff and juniors went to get subsidised lunches. Front-line revenue generators like me would never be seen dead there – we were either chained to our workstations or lunching clients at proper restaurants.

I tried to work out Rory's game plan. It would look good to management – imposing strict economies on the team – and it would look as if there was a strong team spirit – the MD's, as the most senior and well paid team members, picking up the tab for everyone else. What he hadn't said was how much he would be paying personally towards the cost. All MD's were not exactly equal, so would there be an even seven-way split between us or would he shoulder more of the burden? Someone checked with his PA and you can guess the answer.

So anyway, there we were, thirty of us, drinking sparkling wine and serving ourselves with cheap canapés, while making small talk with people we'd sat next to all year, without our spouses (probably doing them a favour), in a room that could seat a hundred and fifty, and was decorated only with some cheap tinsel and baubles. There was no live music – in the past we'd often had live jazz, which definitely hits my spot – and instead the secretaries had brought in CD's of boy-bands I'd never heard of. Luckily the music was so weird that no-one was dancing, so the MD's were excused the need to show what good sports they were by strutting their stuff on the dance floor. The other piece of good news was that the bill at the end of the evening would definitely not be much. No-one could dare to get drunk, in case they said something they shouldn't. Everyone was hanging around Rory, who seemed utterly bored and kept looking at his watch.

At nine o'clock, the evening reached its low point: the juniors had made a

spoof video. This was a tradition on the team, and a kind of competition among the younger team members, to see who could be the most creative and yet risqué at the same time, pushing the envelope in terms of aggression verging on insubordination towards the MD's – except Rory, of course.

Well this year it was different. The lights went down and we all sat around a giant screen TV in the corner of the canteen, drinking more sparkling wine and munching cheese crackers – which by now we were all sick of – and a series of sketches started as the juniors mimicked the idiosyncrasies of the senior team members.

Except that half of the juniors weren't on the team anymore.

It slowly dawned on me – on everyone – that Rory had quietly fired half of them over the previous few weeks. As I looked around, I caught the nervous glances of the few remaining ones, as they saw their old comrades in arms on the screen. It was a cross between a wake and a memorial service. How was it possible that so many young people could quietly disappear in such a short space of time and no-one seemed to notice, let alone comment on it? Were we really so self-absorbed that it simply passed us by? They were real people, after all, they had wanted to be investment bankers, they had worked hard, and now they were… well, they were gone. Afterwards I heard that they had not all been terminated – one had been moved to the library, which is worse than being fired. When it came to an end the lights came up and we all applauded politely and Rory said, 'Well done, everyone,' and left without saying another word. The other MD's took their cue from him and left as soon as he was out of the way.

Bill Myers was fired today. You don't know Bill? I'm not surprised. Bill was the quietest Managing Director on the team, a kind-hearted man approaching fifty years of age, married with four children and always looking as if life had dealt him a bad hand. In the high-flying world of investment banking, Bill was undoubtedly a low-flyer, a turboprop, World War One vintage biplane that had somehow survived because he was vaguely useful and despite his apparent seniority not very expensive. He had been at the firm far too long – nearly eighteen years – and constituted the tribal memory of the team, as well as taking charge of the juniors, training and mentoring them, and looking after some of the duller, less important aspects of the team's work, like monitoring costs. Useful but dull, that was Bill. He commuted every day from somewhere near Brighton and always seemed slightly frayed around the edges. Someone told me he had a handicapped daughter, but I knew that would cut no ice with management. The fact was, Rory could present a senior firing as a decisive act of strong leadership without actually losing much by way of revenue. It would be a pain in the neck for everyone else, because other people would have to pick up some of the administrative and personnel duties that he had handled, but for Rory it was a clear win.

I suppose it was the eighteen years' service that really did for him. If he had been a sharp job-hopper, never more than two or three years in any one firm, moving from one guaranteed package to the next, he'd have been both richer and better regarded. But he hadn't, so he was poorer and largely disregarded. When he arrived in the morning there was a black bin liner sitting on his desk, a note from Personnel and a security guard hanging around 'unobtrusively', making sure he did not do anything stupid like smashing his computer screen.

Not that Bill would ever have done anything like that. Bill could define the term middle-aged: balding, greying, stooping, physically pear-shaped, he did not even look like an investment banker. He saw the bin-liner, went deathly pale, picked up the envelope from Personnel, opened it and read the contents. Then he closed his eyes, breathed a big sigh and looked around at the team, a lost, blank expression on his face.

'So that's it?' He looked sad and lonely as we all stared at our screens and pretended to be making phone calls.

As the guard took Bill's pass and company credit card and mobile phone, I glanced across at Rory's office, to see if he was watching. After eighteen years' service, couldn't Bill expect that his boss would at least do the deed face to face? No – the lights were out and the office was empty.

It was only later, in the gents', that I spoke to Nick Hargreaves.

'He can't have been making more than three hundred. He's a lifer, or very nearly, and they never get paid.'

That was Nick's assessment. I nodded. 'Still, three hundred spread around the MD's would help a little.'

'Nah.' Nick gave a smug grin, as if he was somehow privy to Rory's thinking in a way that I was not. He tapped the side of his nose. 'It's all about positioning. Rory can milk this for a lot more than that. You mark my words.'

I left the gents' with a spring in my step. This was the first good news in weeks.

After Bill's desk had been cleared, I decided to think about Christmas presents. Not for myself, of course – I already felt Bill had given me an unexpected surprise – but for the important people in my life: the clients whose fees pay my bonus. As investment banks' services to their clients get more and more commoditised, and clients find it hard to tell the different banks apart, Bartons has sought to distinguish itself from the rest of the pack. We're the generous bank. We give great gifts to the individuals who run major corporates, and in return, they give us great gifts – of fees for deals they never knew they wanted to do. I think of it as a financial eco-system – we send gifts to the clients, and the clients send us gifts from their shareholders, which in turn pay for more gifts, and so on.

The thing about presents is that you have to pitch them just right. Give too little, and you can actually cause offence, or seem like a cheapskate. On the other hand, if you overdo it, your gift might seem excessive, almost like a bribe, and obviously we'd never bribe anyone. It's in the firm's Code of Practice – we're simply not like that. And what could be even worse, would be if the clients felt obliged to reciprocate, not with business and deals and fees, but with gifts. Who needs gifts? Gifts are for girls. Real men want bonuses.

So I drew up a list of clients and split them into three. The first part of the list was those who really could give me some business, and whose home addresses I knew. The next part was those who really could give me some business, but whose home addresses I hadn't been able to find out. And the third part of the list was those whose home addresses I did know, but who were not in a position to give me any business, although they did know my home address and understood the game.

The best list to be on is the first. A client who really can give you some business is worth cultivating. Not bribing, mind you – cultivating. And if you know his home address, then cultivating him is a lot easier. Gifts that arrive at home obviously ought to be declared by the client to his employer, just in case they were ever to influence him in deciding who to give a piece of business to, but somehow in the hurly-burly of the run-up to Christmas, when there are a thousand and one things to do, some things may be overlooked. Like enormous hampers from Fortnum's, or cases of vintage port, or boxes of Cuban cigars. It's easily done.

The worst part of the list to be on is the second. Gifts delivered to a client's office are subject to whatever regime his firm imposes. Some firms make the recipient donate them to their annual charity auction. Others say the recipient can keep gifts below a certain (ludicrously low) value, but anything beyond that must go into a pool of gifts distributed via a draw at the annual staff party. There's really no point in sending these people anything worthwhile, and so they're the ones who get the desk diaries and the restaurant guides. Later on, when it comes to Ascot and Cowes Week and Wimbledon and Henley, you do your best to make it up to them, but in the meantime Santa's reindeer don't park on their roofs.

The really interesting group are the last one. They're the people who don't have any business to give you, and realise that, but understand how to play the game. They're the ones you can 'entertain' to dinner at a top restaurant without actually troubling them with an invitation or the requirement to attend: they understand. They're the ones you get the bank to buy Wimbledon tickets for without imposing on them the tedious obligation of sitting in those tight little seats in the Centre Court on a hot summer's day. In short, they're the ones who help you out when the in-laws are in town and you need to make a good impression and it's half way through the year and the bonus is still months away, but you're already overdrawn. They're friends.

Friends are people you look after – because they look after you. So the third list get really special, personalised presents – silver coasters from Tiffany, special gift sets of aromatherapy oils from Jo Malone, a humidor from Davidoff. These gifts are the ones I really think about, because in a manner of speaking, I expect to be on the receiving end of 'presents' from these people all year round. And just occasionally, because they know me too, they send me something in return – at home, of course. It's never anything of value, obviously, or I'd disclose it to the Compliance Department, who exist to keep us on the straight and narrow. No commercial value is the phrase – and after all, once a bottle of Macallan forty-year old's been opened, it really doesn't have any commercial re-sale value, does it?

So we all sit at our workstations, making calls, placing orders, working through our Christmas lists. This is the one area where the firm does not cut corners. We might all have to slum it in Business Class on long-haul flights, we might be forced to take public transport out to Heathrow, but we can still stretch the corporate plastic at Fortnums. There's a hum on the desk, a buzz, like I haven't felt in weeks. We're working, and the team spirit really kicks in. Just one big happy family, looking forward to Christmas and all it brings.

After work, a normally pleasant event – someone's leaving drinks. I always feel instinctively good about someone leaving: one less mouth to feed come bonus time. The person leaving – strictly speaking retiring, though he's still a few years away from the official retirement age – is Jeff Ward, one of the longest serving sales-traders on the floor. Jeff is a classic old Stock Exchange figure, a source of advice in difficult situations, a fund of experience such as you rarely find in any firm, and while he does like a drink or two at lunchtime – almost uniquely in the firm, though once it was the norm – his instinct is always to do the right thing. It's as if he's the corporate conscience of the trading floor.

He hasn't had any line management responsibility for some time now, since an unfortunate incident that embarrassed the firm and left everyone feeling slightly uncomfortable. We'd done what's called a block trade – bought a huge holding of shares from a corporate seller with a view to selling them on at a higher price. Jeff didn't want to do the business – he said the price was wrong and the market felt dodgy. Naturally the investment bankers whose client wanted us to do the business tried to downplay his views – they didn't understand what he meant when he said the market 'felt dodgy' and instead produced charts and graphs and trend lines and everyone smiled indulgently at the Old

Man of the Markets who was trying to stand in the way of a lucrative piece of business.

Except he was right.

We bought the shares and tried to sell them on, but over the course of the morning, the market started to fall and soon we realised we were going to be stuck with a large unsold position – so large, in fact, that we would have to disclose it to the Stock Exchange, which would be a disaster, since all of our competitors would know we had it and the price would fall through the floor. Not only would we look like idiots, but we stood to lose millions.

Naturally we had to do something about this, and the first instinct of the investment bankers was to conceal the information internally and work out a game-plan. So far, so good, but one of the people they had to deal with was Jeff, and in the simple world he inhabited, if you took a risk and it went wrong, you paid the price. If the position had to be disclosed, then disclosed it should be. He didn't say 'I told you so', but instead set to work trying to think how to hedge the firm's risk.

In the meantime, the investment bankers decided to lie. Not a Big Lie, of course, just an itsy-witsy, teeny-weeny little lie. They decided to say nothing to the market, on the grounds that the amount of unsold shares was actually small enough not to need disclosure – the balance was sitting on the firm's 'normal trading book' and as a 'normal trading position', wouldn't need to be revealed to anyone. As sleight of hand goes, it was not a bad strategy – though of course I would never be tempted to do anything similar myself – but when Jeff heard, he said no. He said that it was almost certainly wrong from a legal perspective, and if they were caught they could go to prison, but it was definitely wrong morally. Morally? Yes, really – he said that no amount of money made on any one trade could ever justify jeopardising the good name and reputation of the firm, and he went over the investment bankers' heads, directly to Sir Oliver, and laid it on the line.

Of course, Sir Oliver was hugely embarrassed. He was caught between a rock and a hard place, and had no choice but to Do The Right Thing. So the firm disclosed the position, the share price fell, and Jeff worked like a dog to hedge it and work it and eventually, three months later, thanks in part to a buoyant market, the last of the shares were sold, at a modest overall profit.

And do you know what they did? They transferred the investment bankers overseas, and then waited another six months to 're-organise' Jeff's division, removing him from any management or decision-making responsibility. And this year, they were going to fire him – but he was a canny old fox, and somehow a little bird had tipped him off, which is why we had the very unusual spectacle of a retirement drinks party several years before he reached retirement age, and just a few days before the bonus. Jeff was leaving in his own time and on his own terms – with dignity and honour intact.

Naturally, the rest of us felt very uncomfortable. It was not that we wouldn't put pride and reputation first, of course, and after a lifetime in the City, Jeff could probably afford to quit anyway. But fundamentally, we all agreed, he was a dinosaur. He'd been in the City thirty years, man and boy, and was simply out of kilter with the times.

Only this dinosaur had teeth. This dinosaur was an Allosaurus – an Allosaurus with a sore head who was looking for a fight.

We all went into the downstairs bar of the Happy Jobber, one of those traditional bangers and mash, sawdust on the floor, pubs that men of Jeff's generation had always enjoyed, and which had somehow survived the corporatisation of the City and the slow but steady disappearance of men who drank at lunchtime. The place was packed. I suppose there were two hundred of us, from all parts of the firm, including most of the heads of department, and Jeff had his credit card behind the bar so we could take full advantage of his hospitality. At around eight o'clock, Sir Oliver put in an appearance, with Rory in tow, and someone banged a glass for him to say a few well-chosen words.

'Your retirement, Jeff, seems like the passing of an era. When I look around the trading floor today, I see no-one from the same mould as you. Truly, you have been unique and your contribution to the firm has been extraordinary. We shall mark your passing as a defining moment for the firm as we move forward into a different age, a different climate for the City of London...' and so on. I'm not sure he ever actually said he liked Jeff or would miss him, but I'd had a few glasses of champagne and might not have been concentrating. At the end we all clapped politely and then, instead of letting us all carry on drinking, while Sir Oliver and Rory sloped off, Jeff announced that he wanted to say a few words too.

I had no idea what was coming.

'Thank you, Sir Oliver, and thank you all, for coming along tonight. It's good to see so many familiar faces, because it will help me remember what it is I'll be missing from now on, the people I won't be seeing each day. When I first started at Bartons, Sir Oliver was a mere whipper-snapper, the old Chairman's son, brought in to learn the trade.'

At this point, Sir Oliver smiles politely, but I can tell he doesn't mean it. Rory and the other heads of department take their cue from him and put on corporate smiles – polite ones that they don't mean, and which show that they're really just indulging the old codger because it's his last day and he's probably ga-ga and half-cut anyway.

'Ollie the Wally, we called you – wouldn't dare to now, of course.' A few people, who have obviously had one too many already, snigger at this, but then stop as they realise their mistake. Too late, because Rory's clocked them – ouch, it's a bad time of year to be caught laughing at the Chairman. Sir Oliver's smile has become fixed, frozen in place, while Rory and the others have stopped smiling and are glancing around, looking at their watches, doing their best 'I'm bored and I'm not paying attention' impressions. Jeff seems to savour the moment and pauses to take a deep breath, as if by inhaling the moment, he can capture it for the future. There's a twinkle in his eye as he continues. 'But in those days, everyone called you that – even your special friend from Eton, that nice young man with the wavy fair hair who joined with you. Funny – I can picture him now as if it was only yesterday. Very tall, very elegant, with girlish features and delicate hands with long fingers and the family crest on a ring on his pinkie.' Jeff looks at Sir Oliver in a very unusual way, almost as if he's the predator, and Sir Oliver the prey. This makes me very uncomfortable – the investment banking food chain simply doesn't work like this, at least not normally. 'But then Sir Edward sacked him.' Jeff pauses, as if trying to recollect something from far back in his memory, while Sir Oliver stops smiling and stares ahead, tight-lipped. 'Something to do with the Christmas party, and some misunderstanding, as I recall. Something to do with the two of you. And a broom cupboard. Or was it the stationery cupboard? Anyway, that's not important now, is it?' Christ almighty – I stare at the floor, then glance up again at Jeff, trying not to catch anyone else's eye. He's grinning now, staring at Sir Oliver as if to bait him. 'What was his name? I saw him in the paper just the other day. Oh, yes, I remember – he's the Chief Executive of –'

Before Jeff can finish, Sir Oliver steps in front of him and booms out in his loudest, most authoritarian voice, 'Thank you, Jeff, for that little reminder of the past.' He smiles magnanimously, but it's clear that his eyes are as dark as thunder. 'It's funny how these tales can grow in the telling. Ladies and gentlemen, let's have a big round of applause for Jeff.' Even as he's speaking, he starts clapping as loudly as he can, and Rory and the heads of department join in and look around commandingly, so that we all follow suit, and the applause rocks the rafters and drowns out anything else Jeff might have wanted to say. After a vicious glance in Jeff's direction – the sort of glance that would kill me on the spot, but Jeff just grins – Sir Oliver exits while the rest of us try to push our way to the bar for another drink.

Jeff stays rooted to the spot, staring at Sir Oliver's retreating back, then drains

his glass. We're all avoiding him, not wanting to risk being implicated in whatever it was that he just implied about Sir Oliver, aware of the intense scrutiny of Rory and the other hard men from the Executive Compensation Committee, as they search for dissenters, for anyone bold enough even to talk to Jeff, even though it's his retirement party and his credit card that's buying the drinks.

Naturally, we all do the correct thing and ignore him.

FRIDAY, 10TH DECEMBER –
B minus 7

A major shock – Rick Jenkins was fired today. Rick was an Executive Director, a good, solid producer, and everyone thought he was a cast iron certainty to be made up to MD this year, especially after Bill Myers had 'made room' for him. Rick was an operator. Not only had he invited Rory to his wedding last year, but he had even made him godfather to his first child just two months ago. He had the longest Christmas present list on the team, even though he wasn't an MD yet. He really knew how to play the game and work the system, and I'd have sworn he had a great future ahead of him. But Rory had decided his great future was somewhere else.

He was in a state of shock when they walked him out of the building after 'black-bagging' him. He had always talked a good story about how tough he was and the sport he'd done at university, and how he'd personally hang rapists, and any mugger who tried it on with him had better watch out. So I wondered briefly if he would do something outrageous and smash up his desk or trash Rory's office. But he didn't. I suppose executive aggression and the real thing aren't quite the same.

Later, Rory showed up at the desk – he'd been 'held up' in a management committee when Rick was fired – and wandered round, seeing how we all were, taking the temperature of the team and doing a morale-check.

He needn't have bothered. We all smiled great cheesy grins and no-one mentioned Rick. His body could have been lying underneath the desk and we would have pretended it wasn't there. After a few weeks, when the smell got really bad, we'd have sprayed aerosols of air freshener around, but no-one would have said a word. Not before payday.

After lunch, a note went round that there would be an important presentation at 5:00 pm, with attendance required by all executives. Suddenly those stories about the bonus being waived seemed a lot more plausible, although the rumour machine went into overdrive and invented a whole load of new ones too. The favourite was that there was going to be a takeover. Jean-Luc called from Paris to say that one of the big German commercial banks was going to bid for Bartons, and Sir Oliver, as the controlling family shareholder, was selling us out. Don't ask me how he was meant to have heard this in Paris of all places. And then again, if it was true, would it be good news? Would the incoming owners be anxious to ensure continuing staff goodwill and increase the bonus pool – yes, some people really wondered about this – adding some long-term incentive payments to keep us all locked in, or would they announce wholesale redundancies, closing entire business areas, on the grounds that it's a buyer's market for jobs out there and most of us would rather have any job – even without a bonus – than find ourselves on the street?

We filed into the large presentation room on the ground floor and took our places. There was a podium at the front of the room where Sir Oliver was sitting with several heads of department, including Rory. They were all smiling, as if they had some really good news to tell us. This made us all extremely worried. When it seemed as if everyone who could be crammed into the room was there – it seated nearly five hundred, and there was standing room only at the back – Sir Oliver stood up and went to the microphone.

'Ladies and gentlemen – welcome.' He smiled magnanimously around the room. 'It's good to see so many familiar faces here today.' Don't bullshit us – there are several hundred fewer faces because of your pre-bonus cost-cutting. 'Today I have great pleasure in making a significant announcement that will affect all of our futures.' Oh Christ, he's sold the bloody bank. 'Today the board of the bank, under my chairmanship, has taken a major decision.' The board – shit – this is it: the real thing. 'The Management Committee has been fully involved in this decision and briefed upon it at every stage of the way, and is unanimously behind the move.' Bullshit – all that means is that they've been bought off. 'Ladies and gentlemen, after a hundred and fifty years, the board of Bartons has decided –' Oh God, let it be good news, please. '– to re-brand the bank.' There's an audible sigh of relief around the room. Imagine five hundred people taking a deep breath, holding it until they're going purple, and then releasing it in a single rush, almost like a collective orgasm. 'After a hundred and fifty years of honest, reliable service to our clients, of being known for the quality of our work and the integrity of our people, we have decided it is appropriate to move with the times. We live in an age of image projection, sound bites, spin doctors, advertising and marketing. We must adapt. So ladies and gentlemen, following an eight month intensive programme of brainstorming, research, focus groups, visual identity development and brand testing, I am proud to present: the new Bartons, Bartons for the twenty-first century!'

Incredibly, the SurroundSound speakers in the conference room blare out a trumpet fanfare, and on the screen behind him the word 'Bartons' appears, but in a new typeface and coloured gold, rather than our traditional dark green. An American voice-over introduces 'Bartons, an investment bank for the twenty-first century – Bartons, the bank that's trying harder – trying to succeed.' Yes, really. The whole time we were sweating our guts out, desperately killing ourselves over the bonus, watching as old colleagues were black-bagged, looking on as poor Bill Myers was taken out and shot, the management were working with a branding agency, spending God knows what to change the colour of our stationery. The scene becomes even more surreal as girls from a PR agency walk down the aisles, handing out T-shirts and baseball caps with the new corporate logo – 'Bartons – we're really trying' – and all the time trumpets are sounding and the American voice-over talks about our corporate values, our noble history and our fine traditions, all of which sit so happily with a spirit of entrepreneurialism and innovation for the twenty-first century. And do you know what we do?

We cheer.

Yes, really – none of the polite, measured applause you'd expect from socially inhibited English people – we get up out of our seats and we cheer, with great grins on our faces. Partly it's relief that we haven't been sold, but mostly it's knee-jerk sycophancy, always the safe default position in the presence not only of the board, but so many of one's peers as well. Some people are giving each other high fives, normally sober colleagues hug each other and slap each other on the back, and the room echoes with the noise of our exuberance and enthusiasm.

On the podium, Sir Oliver looks at his colleagues and nods. Rory nods back. They were right. We really are a bunch of sheep.

I took a day off sick today.

Before you say anything, I know that investment bankers, in their capacity as masters of the universe, are not allowed ever to get sick. Illness is a sign of weakness, and weakness is a vice allowed only to the competition.

The reason I took this unprecedented step is that after one of the worst weekends in living memory, I did not sleep at all last night. I literally stayed up all night, pacing around, convinced that if I went in to work, I would be the one to be black-bagged.

Wendy was beside herself. She accused me of being crazy – she actually said mentally unbalanced, when in fact I'm the most rational person I know – and if it was going to be me, at least let's find out now, rather than later. She said that running away and hiding achieved nothing, and how on earth had we got ourselves trapped in this worthless life.

You can imagine what I said to that. Worthless? How many other women get to wear twenty thousand pounds worth of jewellery to a dinner party? How many get taken to Glyndebourne, Covent Garden, Garsington, Ascot, Henley and Wimbledon every single year, and always at someone else's expense? How many get to shop at Harrods and Selfridges and Fortnum and Mason and run up credit card bills of thousands of pounds every month?

And do you know what she said? She actually said she didn't care about all that, it was like a bad drug habit (how would she know?) and she'd kick it in a second if we could only walk away from all this.

She said she'd never been happier than when we were first married and living in a rented flat in Battersea, eating takeaway pizza and drinking cheap red wine.

I just about went berserk. Cheap red wine? Who the fuck drinks cheap red wine? No-one we know, anyway.

But that wasn't the end of it. There was more. She asked me if I could remember when I last gave her a hug! You can imagine what I said to that. Anyone can give their wife a hug – but how many men give their wives two thousand pound Bulgari bracelets for their birthday? Or three hundred pound bouquets of flowers on their anniversary? Or bring them back a five thousand dollar kimono when they come back from a business trip to Tokyo – and before you say anything, yes I was feeling a little guilty after that trip, and I did charge it to expenses, but that's hardly the point, is it?

When I'd calmed down, and she'd stopped crying and admitted that yes, she understood that I did all this for her, and she'd been confused and foolish and I should ignore her stupid remarks earlier, there was no way I could sleep and so I stayed up and eventually watched the dawn over the rooftops of London, which was very gratifying, reminding me why a top floor flat in Sloane Square commands such a premium.

The problem was, by morning I looked like shit and felt even worse. When I rang my number, Nick Hargreaves picked up the line.

'Nick… it's me,' I croaked.

'Who?'

'Me – Dave. I'm feeling awful. Must be a bug of some kind. I've been throwing up all night.'

There was a silence at the other end. Not a good silence, an embarrassed, awkward silence. A long pause, and then: 'Will you be in later?'

'No. Not the way I'm feeling. Is there any special reason, Nick? Is there anything I should know?'

Another long silence. 'I guess nothing that can't wait. See you tomorrow. Get your strength back.' He hung up before I could say anything. 'Get your strength back'? No-one tells you to 'get your strength back' when you're ill. They say things like 'get well soon', or 'I hope you're feeling better tomorrow'. Why should I need my strength? What does he know that I don't? Is there a black bin-liner sitting on my desk with a letter from Personnel?

I put my head in my hands and almost started to cry.

It was only much later, around eleven o'clock, when I woke up on the couch in the study and went in search of Wendy. She looked tired too, and stepped away when I tried to put my arms around her waist and kiss her.

'Please don't.' There was a tightness to her, a fragility that I hadn't noticed before.

'Okay, I'm sorry. Let's just put last night behind us. It's almost over now. I'm going to take a shower, shave and go out for a breath of air.'

She looked relieved as I headed off to the bathroom.

When I was ready, I stepped out into Sloane Street and headed off, walking aimlessly as I enjoyed an unusually pleasant winter's day, with a clear blue sky and a crisp coldness in the air that sent shivers right through me, chasing away the fatigue of the previous night. I walked and walked, much further than I'd intended, and eventually found myself in Piccadilly. I stopped briefly at the Fountain Restaurant in Fortnum's for a light lunch and a glass of wine, feeling strangely exuberant, like a child playing truant from school. Afterwards I wandered off around the side streets of St James's until I found myself, just after two o'clock, outside Christie's.

The Africa sale had just started.

You know what happened next.

Afterwards, when I emerged once more onto the pavement, it was already getting dark. The air was damp as well as chilly, and I hurried to find a cab to carry my purchases home, thinking how I would explain to Wendy that I'd just blown nearly five grand on a bunch of nineteenth century relics of the Great Age of Exploration.

I went in two hours early today. I was at my workstation at five-thirty, while the cleaners were still vacuuming, and searched everywhere for evidence of either a black bin-liner or an envelope from Personnel. When I was sure there was nothing waiting for me – I even checked the contents of my drawers three times – I looked on everyone else's desks, checked their drawers and then tried Rory's office, though that was locked. Nothing. I wondered then if Nick had been playing some cruel trick on me yesterday, trying to spook me. Or maybe someone else had gone. I looked around, but none of the other workstations looked particularly vacant.

There was a time, about two years ago, when someone played a cruel trick at Hardman Stoney, during the annual cull to thin out the headcount immediately prior to bonus, and placed a black bin-liner and an empty sealed envelope on a colleague's desk. It was meant to be a laugh, a hysterical, quite near the knuckle, risqué joke. But it backfired. The individual concerned arrived, saw the bin-liner and the envelope, threw the bin-liner on the floor and took the envelope into the Heads of Department meeting, where his boss was discussing the business of the day ahead with his opposite numbers from around the bank. He grabbed his boss, pinned him to the table, and tried to shove the envelope down his throat. You can imagine what happened next. By the time he was restrained, and what was left of the empty envelope had been opened, his team had removed the bin-liner – doubtless fearing the worst – and swore blind that they knew nothing about whatever it was he was alleging. He was summarily dismissed, of course, saving his boss another tough decision ahead of their annual payday. As they say on Wall Street, all's fair in love and the bonus round.

I hung around, drinking coffee from the machine, waiting for the others to arrive, and all the time wondering if Nick had been playing something similar on me. Interestingly, he was the first to arrive, and smirked when he saw me, though he wasn't obviously carrying a spare bin-liner to place on my desk.

'You're in early – must have made a full recovery?'

I could have killed him. It actually occurred to me to leap across the desk at him, put my hands around his throat and keep squeezing until his eyes popped out of their sockets and he stopped breathing forever.

Instead I just smiled. 'Much better, thanks. Thought I'd make an early start and catch up. How was yesterday?'

You may find this hard to believe, but I am capable of being both devious and ruthless. Which brings me to my revenge on Nick. I sat seething all morning, thinking of different ways to torture and humiliate him. Just as I was finishing a particularly exquisite fantasy, in which I was appointed Rory's deputy with specific responsibility for compensation and expense monitoring, his boyfriend called. His boyfriend is an interior designer called Charles. I've only met him once, and he struck me as a really nice guy. Naturally that wouldn't stop me getting my revenge.

I only caught one side of the conversation, but it was enough to realise that they were meeting after work for a drink with some friends, and his other half would be downstairs at 7:30 pm.

So I ordered flowers. Flowers? Sure – a huge arrangement, a hundred pounds worth, lilies and white roses, to be delivered to Nick, here on the trading floor, unsigned, but with the message, 'The earth moved for me' and lots of kisses. He was amazed when they arrived, just before six, and one of the security guards brought them over to his workstation amidst much cat-calling and whistling from the traders. When he looked at the message, he went bright red, and looked very unsure of himself. I thought to myself, do you have some guilty secrets, or what? So at seven-fifteen I went down to reception, hung around until I spotted Charles, went over and re-introduced myself, and asked if he was there to meet Nick. When he said he was, I invited him up to the trading floor, and swiped him through the security turnstiles on my card, so that I could take him up to our floor and over to the team area. When he got there, Nick was on the phone to a client in the States, and since I made sure we approached from behind, he never spotted us, until his boyfriend tapped him on the shoulder and grinned.

Nick's face was a picture.

And then I said to Charles, 'What fantastic flowers'. He looked puzzled, and with Nick looking on nervously, still stuck on the phone and unable to stop him, he picked up the card that was lying next to the bouquet.

The thing about revenge is that it can be the sweetest feeling. And when it comes after what has really been a gruesome time, it tastes sweeter still. So when Charles turned bright red with anger, picked up the flowers, hit Nick over the head with them not once, but seven – yes, seven – times, and stormed off, snarling over his shoulder that Nick needn't bother to come home, it was a huge effort on my part to retain my dignity and not to double up laughing. When Nick finally finished his call, he picked up his jacket from the back of his chair, threw a horribly accusing glance in my direction, and rushed after his partner.

Now is that devious, or what? Not as devious as what came a few minutes later, when I wandered over to Rory's office to ask his PA (in a suitably loud voice – Rory was sitting at his desk) if she knew where Nick was, because his jacket was gone from his chair and a client in Chicago needed him urgently.

Now that is devious.

It's almost over, at least for another year. Tomorrow is Bonus Day. The day after tomorrow, the day when We All Know, the start of another year, well… that's B minus 365.

Yesterday I caught Rory staring at me from his office. He looked away, turned to some papers spread out on the desk in front of him, shook his head and scratched something out with his pen.

This was very unsettling, but not nearly as unsettling as what happened next. Nick was fired!

It was the last thing any of us expected, obviously including him, because even by investment banking standards, firing someone on the day before bonus is pretty brutal.

But Nick had been a naughty boy, and someone had tipped off the Compliance Department, the internal 'police' who keep us on the straight and narrow. Nick had been dealing in shares.

Now, before you say anything – yes, it was Nick's job, in a manner of speaking, to deal in shares. But these were illicit dealings, unauthorised by the Compliance Department, for his own account. The earlier rumours had actually been true, though I would never have imagined that Nick would be the guilty party. He had opened a personal dealing account with another broker, based in Geneva, and had been using inside information to profit at the expense of our own clients. When he heard a big purchase order was coming in to buy a particular company's shares, he quickly bought some of the shares in question himself, for his own account, and then waited for the big purchase to push the price up higher, making him a tidy profit. Quite illegal, of course, it's called dealing ahead of a client. It was common practice in the old days, but today we're all too ethical to do this stuff – unless, like Nick, we're in such a hurry that we're willing to break the rules.

So who'd have thought it? Rory's blue-eyed boy is escorted off the floor to an interview room, where the police are waiting to talk to him. Now, normally I wouldn't spare a second thought for the dear old boys in blue, who after all earn next to nothing compared to investment bankers, and funnily enough don't live in top floor apartments around Sloane Square or eat at Colon, but this time I really admire them and wonder how they actually caught him. Apparently they were put onto him by an anonymous tip-off, but who could have known? Certainly not me, or I wouldn't have bothered to play the flower trick on him – I'd have done for him this way instead. Privately, I'm relieved, because I know he knew it was me, and he would have wanted his revenge too, and these things have a way of getting out of hand – turning into vendettas. Publicly, I'm delighted. We all are – think about it. Any nervousness that I felt about tomorrow evaporates as I think what Nick might have made. He looked as if he was onto a winner, he'd been so far up Rory's arse for the past month that only his ankles were showing, and now that money is up for grabs. This could be a great year.

Then comes the bad news. Jean-Luc calls to say that Rory could be in trouble. Where he gets his information I can only guess, but word spreads across the floor like wildfire. Nick is going to be charged. He'll probably go to prison. There'll be no cover-up on this one, they're looking for someone to make an example of – and Nick has just been volunteered.

Can you imagine, an investment banker going to prison? It's absurd. Even Nick doesn't deserve that – prison is for other people, ordinary people: criminals. But anyway, Rory now has to see Sir Oliver to account for what's happened. He's brought the reputation of the bank into disrepute – in a hundred and fifty years, nothing like this has ever happened before. Or at any rate, no-one's been caught, which must say something for the calibre of people we hire.

Our moral standards are of the highest and our reputation is our greatest asset – at least that's what it says on the corporate website. Worst of all, Rory's judgement may be called into question. All of the numbers might have to be re-visited. This is terrible.

On the other hand, it could be great. What if Rory gets fired? What if his enormous share of the bonus pool is up for grabs? What if the board needs to find a successor in a hurry? I could do that job – and if I don't, someone else will. I glance around the desk. Has it occurred to anyone else? Let's hope not.

Cometh the moment, cometh the man. With trembling fingers, I dial Sir Oliver's number. Amazingly, his PA says she'll put me straight through. There's a click and a faint background noise that tells me I'm on a speakerphone. Jesus, I'm playing for high stakes, but fuck it, you only live once. As I'm about to introduce myself and ask for a meeting so that I can formally offer to step into the breach and lead the team forward, a gravelly, older voice growls at me, 'Were you after me or Rory, who's sitting here beside me?'

Then Rory's voice cuts across him, 'What is it, Dave?'

I hold the phone away from me and stare at it. It's another nightmare. It can't be real. Why hasn't Wendy shaken me awake yet? What is it with me and phones?

I hang up.

I cannot believe I did that. What if they call back? What about when Rory returns to the desk and asks what that was all about? What if they're re-doing the bonus numbers right now and I've blown it? I might just have blown a million pounds.

I run for the gents' to be sick.

Later, much later, I emerge cautiously and sneak a look at Rory's office. He's in there, talking to his P.A., dictating something, I think. I walk boldly back to my workstation to resume pretending to work. A flashing light blinks at me and I pick up my phone. I freeze as I recognise Rory's voice and turn to see him staring at me from his office.

'Dave, could you join me for a moment, please?'

I nod, gulp, swallow air, and finally, because I can't actually speak, raise a thumbs up in his direction and hang up. I do my deep breathing exercises, but I'm already sweating as I make my way towards his office, my mind a turmoil as I desperately grope for some kind of rational explanation for my idiocy.

For a ridiculous moment, I wonder whether to tell him the truth. He's a lousy boss and I think I could do better. I really do. You don't doubt that, do you? Success in this business is all about confidence. We're all stark naked all of the time, but some get away with it and some don't. I could get away with it, if only I got the break.

But not today.

Today I open the office door and try to do an engaging grin – which emerges as a toothy sneer – while Rory's PA brushes past me, contempt oozing from her every pore.

'Don't sit down.'

I stop and stare at him. This is not a good start. He's busy studying columns of names and figures – bonus numbers.

'Dave – what was that call you made to Sir Oliver while I was there?'

'C... call?'

'Yes.'

'Oh, you mean that call.'

He puts his pen down, looks up and nods. He's poker-faced, impossible to read. 'Which call did you think I meant?'

At this point I want the ground to swallow me up. 'I... I was after you.'

'Me? What for? Why didn't you wait until I got back?'

'I wanted to catch you before you went in. But Sir Oliver's PA put me straight through. I d... don't know why she did that. I –'

'Why did you want to catch me before I went in?'

All sorts of stupid thoughts fly through my mind – and this time I can't say I wanted to offer him tickets to the soccer or the rugby or the opera or the mud wrestling or any damned corporate entertainment opportunity. 'I… I wanted to say good luck. That was all.'

The effect is amazing. He rocks back in his chair, a look of utter bafflement on his face. I'm helped in part by the fact that the words come out very quietly – because I'm shitting myself – and sound sincere. Now, on the whole, investment bankers don't do sincere – at least not with each other. We do sincere with clients, when we're pleading for business, begging for fees, swearing undying loyalty and total commitment, but we don't actually mean it. This time, I sound as if I mean it, and Rory is completely thrown. He may never have come across a situation like this before and his face betrays a mixture of emotions – gratitude, quickly replaced by suspicion, followed by guilt (about my bonus number? – Aaaaargh!) and finally bewilderment: this does not compute. He coughs.

'Thank you, Dave. I appreciate it. I really do. In fact everything's fine. Sir Oliver's very supportive and we've agreed a press release. As far as the team's concerned, it's business as usual.'

'That's great, Rory. No-one's more delighted than I am.'

Great. I'm doing well – in fact better than just well. I'm doing fantastically. And so of course I have to blow it.

'Rory – one thing just occurs to me. What will happen to Nick's – ?'

I don't get the chance to finish the sentence, because Rory goes bright red and explodes with anger.

'IS THAT WHAT THIS WAS ALL ABOUT? DO YOU NEVER THINK OF ANYTHING ELSE?'

I think there may be a few people on the far side of the trading floor, possibly somewhat deaf and in need of new batteries for their hearing aids, who don't actually hear Rory's response. But on reflection I'm probably wrong.

I shrug, desperate once again for the right response.

'Well, it is that time of year…'

'GET OUT!!!'

I run. I don't mean I walk at a brisk pace while trying to preserve my dignity – I mean run. I don't even bother going back to my workstation to collect my jacket or my briefcase. I couldn't have moved faster if there was a T. Rex on my tail, or a Lottery jackpot ticket lying unclaimed at the other end of the trading floor. And where do I run? To the gents', to hide in a cubicle and cry, silently, so that no-one else can hear me. Around nine o'clock that evening I sneak back to the trading floor, after checking that everyone's gone, get my things and go home to sob my heart out with Wendy.

Today has not been a good day – and it's not over yet.

When I get home, the flat's in darkness. I call out to Wendy, check in the kitchen, the dining room and the bedroom. The message light is flashing on the answer-phone, so I press the Play button. It's Jean-Luc, his voice sounding remarkably cheerful as he says there's a rumour going round the Paris office that I've been fired. I hit the Delete button and tiptoe into Samantha's room, which is empty. Finally I spot an envelope on my desk in the study. It has one word written on it, in ink, in Wendy's unmistakably childlike writing – _Dave_. She's underlined it as if to emphasise the finality of whatever it contains, and I pour myself a whisky before sitting down to read it.

She's gone.

But you knew that, didn't you? She's left me for someone else, someone who has become very close to her in recent months, and she wants to start again with him. They're going to lead a different life together from the one we had – a simpler, easier, better life. All she wants from me is the flat, the car, half the bonus, half the proceeds when I eventually get my hands on my options and unvested shares, maintenance for herself and Samantha – whom she'll allow me to see on alternate weekends – and whatever else her lawyer recommends. Oh, and I'll have to pay her legal expenses. She hopes I'll understand, she's not trying to be unreasonable, but the pressure was too much, and she wants to turn her back on material things and be with a man who truly loves and understands her. She's already taken her clothes, her jewellery, some pictures and other bits and pieces of artwork, the car, and 'as a precaution' has drawn some money from the bank – increasing the overdraft. She hopes we can do this amicably, if only for Samantha's sake, because it's her we should think of first and foremost.

Shit.

But she's right of course. I'd be lying if I said our marriage had been the greatest ever union of two people, and it's not as if I haven't occasionally – well, you know – but as it sinks in I feel a curious mixture of emotions: relief, that now I can go out and get laid whenever I want; concern that people might think I've somehow failed; anger that she's going to rip me off financially in what seems certain to be a terrible year; optimism that I can effectively trade her for a younger, more beautiful, more amenable model; outrage at what she's already taken – including my daughter, my own flesh and blood – and ultimately despair, because even my resolution and capacity for rationalising any setback are finally exhausted. I've lost my wife and daughter. I've lost my right hand, my trusted aide and confidante, my ally as I fought my way through the corporate jungle. She was the reason I did all this – well, her and the money and the lifestyle. I'll probably lose my home and most of my possessions, and with my bonus prospects down the toilet, I just can't see how I'm going to dig my way out of this one. Forget Barbados, forget the Porsche, forget the makeover for the flat – in fact forget the flat altogether. I'll have to go and live somewhere terrible like Fulham. When I look around me the brutal finality of it all sinks in. I feel physically sick. It's over.

How could she do this to me? I gave her everything – everything – a woman could want. Well, maybe not an actual place in the country, and okay, the flat's not as nice as the Finkelsteins', but we would have got there. At least I didn't make her live in Balham like Bob and Trish Harris. And I know that Wendy would have looked great cruising down the King's Road on a sunny day in the 911, with the top down, wearing her Gucci shades. There's a new range of brushed gold jewellery from Tiffany that she would have looked amazing in – I already had my eye on the necklace and ear-rings as a post-bonus surprise for her. And then there's Barbados. She always loved Barbados.

I'd like to say that I cried myself to sleep, curled up in a ball on her side of the bed, sniffing her perfume on the pillow.

But of course I don't. I decide that activity is key, so I check the tickets for Barbados and leave a message on the answer-phone at the travel agents, asking if hers is transferable, and start thinking who I might take in her place. Then I call round the various credit card firms to cancel her cards, and leave another message for the bank. On a whim, I phone the police and tell them the car's been stolen – that should be worth a laugh in the morning. And finally I go to the storeroom where she kept her mementoes of childhood and schooldays boxed up in an old chest, and take the whole lot down to the basement and tip it into the rubbish skip. It's not exactly progress, I know, but at least it keeps me from hitting the bottle. It's not yet midnight, and I'm all alone, worn out, and desperately in need of a good night's sleep before tomorrow.

So naturally I hit the bottle.

One whisky becomes two, two turn into three, and soon a nearly new bottle is empty. And then, when I should be at my lowest point, when lesser men would be thinking of despair or even suicide, from deep inside me comes a strength I never knew I had. This is not it. I know I have to carry on, I can't give up now, because people like me simply don't do that, and while I still have the presence of mind to do so, I set the alarm for tomorrow morning before passing out sobbing on the sofa.

Even in my sleep, I'm troubled. She's left me for a fucking personal trainer. How shallow is that? Mind you, it could have been worse. In my dreams, my tortured mind plays tricks on me. What if it was Matt Finkelstein? Or Bob 'Fat Man' Harris? Or Jean-Luc? Or Rory... Or all of them...

Thursday, 16th December –
Bonus Day

I wake at 4:00 am, well before the alarm, and start pacing round the flat in the darkness. My mind's a blur of racing, crazy thoughts. I check the answer-phone three times for messages from Wendy. Nothing. I call her mobile, but it's turned off, and I don't want to leave a message. I stand in front of the mirror, naked, and stare at myself. Overnight I seem to have aged about five years. My hair is wildly tangled, streaked with grey that I never seemed to notice before. My eyes are bloodshot from a combination of whisky and tears. My hands are shaking. I think that perhaps I'm going mad. I won't ask what you think.

I steel myself. Today is Bonus Day. The most important day of the year. As they say in the movies, this is not a drill. It's the real thing, and I have to get in early. Get in early and be on the phone, talking to a client – a real one, if I can find one that early, maybe someone in Hong Kong or Singapore – and avoid eye contact with any of the surviving members of the team. There's no point in not showing up at all, because if there's a chance, for the sake of one day and a little more humiliation, I might as well collect whatever's coming my way.

I ignore the empty flat, my aching head and back, and force myself to take a shower and get ready for work.

And then there's my briefcase. I want to get in early to get my briefcase under my workstation without anyone asking what's in it or why I don't just leave it open on the desk where it usually sits.

Today's the day, and there's no reason not to.

When Rory comes in, half an hour later than usual, I have final confirmation that I've blown it. Yesterday was the last nail in my coffin. He sweeps past me, makes polite remarks to a couple of the others, then goes to his office and closes the door. After a few minutes, his PA takes his coffee in, and when she re-appears, she has a list of timings for us each individually to see Rory to get paid for the year. He's left me till last, making me wait until he's seen everyone else on the team, even the juniors – hanging me out to dry, no doubt to savour the moment. I look up, catch his eye and he curls his lip disdainfully.

Well, that's it. I've had enough.

I cough nervously, glance around at my colleagues who all have their eyes glued to the screens in front of them, and pick up my briefcase from under my desk, leaving my jacket over the back of my chair. But you know all this, don't you? You know how I walk over to Rory's office, in a sort of lop-sided way, half concealing my briefcase from the watching eyes of the team, go in, close the door behind me and draw the blinds. You know how this makes him look up, puzzled.

'What are you doing?'

I smile, reassuring, ingratiating.

'Rory, there's… something I wanted to discuss with you.'

He sighs and looks at his watch. 'Okay, I'll give you five minutes, but do me a favour – no more special pleading about the bonus, okay?'

'No, no more special pleading, Rory,' I smile. For an awful, tantalising moment, a voice inside my head seems to be saying that this isn't inevitable, it doesn't really have to happen this way. There is an alternative. But then my eyes fall on the paper in front of him, a list of names ordered to match the sequence of meetings. The name at the bottom is easy to read, because it's mine.

Twenty five thousand pounds.

I glance quickly up the list. Rory doesn't even attempt to cover it up. He wants me to know that mine's the smallest number. A number so small that no Managing Director in the history of the firm has ever been paid so little. In this business, size really does matter. Even the juniors are getting more than me. It would be kinder to fire me.

I smile and shake my head as I rest my briefcase on his desk and flick the catches to open it.

'No, Rory – no more pleading at all.'

First published in Great Britain by

Elliott & Thompson Ltd
27 John Street
London WC1N 2BX

ISBN 1 904027 31 8

First edition

Book design by Brad Thompson
Printed and bound in England by Cambridge Printing